FALLING
FOR
MAPLEWICK

A Maplewick Novel

Wallace Yovetich

Hearthlight Press, Los Angeles

Falling for Maplewick

© 2025 Wallace Yovetich

This is a work of fiction. Names, characters, places, and incidents are products of the author's imagination or are used fictitiously. Any resemblance to actual persons, living or dead, events, or locales is entirely coincidental.

Cover design by Wallace Yovetich
created with Canva

Published by Hearthlight Press
www.wallaceyovetich.com

ISBN: 979-8-9932818-0-3

For Smith, because everything is.

Chapter One

The first sound of morning was the soft hiss of the kettle on the stove.

Mavis Whitlock moved quietly through the kitchen in the apartment above her bookshop, cardigan wrapped loosely around her and sleep still lingering behind her eyes. Outside the window, the rooftops of Maplewick were edged in fog, chimney smoke curling up into the pale blue sky. Somewhere below, a crow muttered its opinion of the morning.

She spooned tea leaves into her favorite strainer—enameled in deep green and chipped at the handle—then filled her mug and leaned against the counter as the steam rose.

The apartment was small and warm and comfortably cluttered. Books in every corner, lined up or lying flat. Max's latest art project was still drying on the kitchen table, and her own well-worn notebook of shop ideas was splayed open beside the toaster, filled with scribbled titles and the occasional recipe idea Ruth had insisted she write down.

She took a slow sip of tea, then looked toward the back of the apartment. Silence. Max was still asleep.

The quiet held. Soft and golden and full of promise.

A creak came from the stairwell behind her, down the back steps that led to the bookshop.

"Hattie," Mavis murmured, not unkindly. "It's too early to haunt anything."

There was no reply, but the faintest scent of old paper drifted up the stairs—her ghostly shopkeeper's way of saying good morning. The creak didn't come again.

She finished her tea, pulled her hair into a loose knot, and grabbed Max's sweatshirt from the back of a chair to bring downstairs. His mornings weren't complete without it, even in August.

❧ ❧ ❧

Downstairs, the shop still slept.

No bell above the door, no footfalls yet on the cobbled path outside. Just the hush of books breathing in their sleep, and the gentle scent of dried lavender tucked in small vases along the windowsills.

Mavis turned on the lamps—warm pools of light flowing over shelves and tabletops. The secondhand section had shifted again. Hattie always rearranged the poetry first.

On the worktable in the back room, a worn history of New England towns lay open to the page on Maplewick. She knew this book. In fact, she hadn't seen it in years—it had belonged to her grandmother, passed down and kept tucked away in the shop's small archive.

It wasn't one that appeared without reason.

The gilt lettering on the spine had faded to a soft green, and the map on the facing page showed the town as it had been in 1821. A sprig of lavender marked the margin beside a paragraph about the original square. Mavis ran her fingers over the page, wondering why Hattie had brought it out now.

"Planning on giving me a history lesson?" she asked softly.

There was a pause in the air—then the faintest shape shimmered near the edge of her vision, the sense of someone standing just behind her shoulder.

"You'll see," came the voice, warm and amused.

Mavis arched her brow. "Cryptic this early in the morning?"

Another whisper of movement, like skirts brushing past, and the lavender sprig shifted half an inch on the page.

"Fine," she said, closing the book gently but leaving it where it was. "I'll bite later."

❧ ❧ ❧

She slipped through the archway into Maple & Sage, her sister's bakery and tea shop, which shared a wall and a dutch-door with her own shop. The change in atmosphere was instant—where her shop was hushed and book-scented, this space was warm and alive. Yeast and cinnamon filled the air, honeyed steam from the teapots clinging to the windows. The morning rush hadn't begun yet, but a low hum of movement was already building in the kitchen beyond. Mavis left the top half of the door open, which was their custom during business hours.

Ruth stood at the counter in flour-dusted linen, cheeks flushed, hair pinned up in a way that never quite worked but always looked like her. She was already halfway through a batch of scones and talking to someone unseen in the back.

When she spotted Mavis, she grinned.

"You look like you argued with your teacup."

"I won," Mavis said, voice still low with sleep. "Barely."

"You want your usual?"

Mavis nodded. "And Max's. He'll be down in a few."

Ruth grabbed two almond scones from the cooling rack and slid them onto a plate. As she did, the scent seemed to soften the room—her subtle kitchen magic wrapping itself around the food. "Susan's already taken the kids to the kitchen with her. Tell Max he can come wreak sugar havoc when he's ready."

Mavis accepted the tea with both hands. It was perfect—black with orange peel and something faintly spicy, just as she liked it.

"You rearranged the shelves again," Ruth said casually, glancing through the shared door.

"Hattie did."

"Mm." Ruth leaned on the counter, her eyes twinkling. "You're the only person I know who can blame anything about their store on a ghost and mean it."

Mavis smiled into her cup.

Back in the shop, the first customer of the day was already browsing—mug from Maple & Sage in hand, a familiar rhythm. The shops had long ago agreed: books could go into the bakery, and tea could come into the bookshop. Maplewick thrived on softness like that. The two stores had been joined since Mavis and Ruth's parents had run them both before handing them down to their daughters.

Max appeared in the doorway a few minutes later, fully dressed but still pillow-faced, hair in chaotic tufts that leaned in every direction.

He blinked at her. "Did you steal my sweatshirt?"

"It was hanging on the back of a chair."

"It was emotionally important to me."

"I was emotionally cold," she said, handing it over.

He tugged it on and yawned. "Is there tea?"

Mavis slid the paper bag and to-go cup across the counter toward him. "From Aunt Ruth. Scone and mint tea."

He climbed onto the stool beside the register and unwrapped the scone with reverence. "Yum, Aunt Ruth is the very best."

"She is," Mavis agreed. "Don't tell your mom," she added with a wink.

Max grinned around a bite. "You're the best too, mom." He said with a full mouth.

They sat together in the quiet of the shop while it fully woke up around them—pages rustling, sunlight pooling slowly across the wood floor, the occasional sound of a customer entering Ruth's side for coffee and cinnamon rolls.

"Is today the presentation at school?" Mavis asked.

Max shrugged. "It's just my ecosystem project."

"Which you've worked on for two weeks."

"Which I will be presenting in front of twenty-nine other humans. I'm trying not to think about it."

She reached over and squeezed his arm. "You'll do great."

He nodded, eyes on the bag that once held the scone, as if he wished there were just one more bite.

Outside, footsteps sounded on the side path. A voice—bright, laughing. Then another. The cousins were on their way.

Max slid off the stool. "They're here."

"Jacket," Mavis reminded him.

"It's August."

"It's Maplewick."

He pulled on his raincoat with dramatic flair, grabbed his backpack, and kissed her cheek in one smooth motion. "Love you. Bye. Try not to let the Hattie alphabetize the titles again."

"I make no promises."

From the front window, Mavis watched as Max joined his cousins—Benji and Grace—at the corner. Susan was there too, holding a thermos and wearing boots that didn't match. She smiled when she saw Mavis in the window and lifted her mug in greeting.

Mavis waved back and stood there for a long moment after they were gone, holding her own cup, the steam rising up toward her face like breath.

Outside, the morning unfurled slowly across the town, and the bookshop settled in to wait for whoever might need it next.

Chapter Two

Julian Everett adjusted his bag for the fourth time in ten minutes, which didn't make it lighter or more comfortable, but gave his hands something to do. The strap kept catching on his corduroy blazer—an unfortunate fashion choice given the warm morning sun—but he couldn't seem to let go of the habit. Corduroy made him feel like a serious researcher. Which, today, he needed.

Maplewick was not what he had expected.

He'd read the town's Wikipedia page. Twice. He'd clicked through a few historic preservation grants and squinted at archival photos from the early 1900s. What he hadn't expected was how quiet it was in person. Not empty. Just... content. Like the town had already exhaled and was happy to let you catch up.

The Maplewick Inn sat at the edge of the town square, all gables and ivy and long windows with flower boxes under them. A brass plaque near the door read: Established 1787 — Restored 1974 — Loved Ever Since. The front garden was more wildflowers than landscaping, and the gravel path crunched under his boots as he stepped up to the porch.

The inn looked like it had once been a large house—rambling and gently lopsided with age, but clearly cared for. A low wooden swing hung from the porch. There was a ceramic bowl of water beside the steps for dogs. On the windowsill above the front door, someone had tucked a pinecone and two feathers like an offering.

The front door opened before he could knock.

"You must be Julian," the woman on the other side greeted him warmly.

She was in her forties, dressed in soft linen pants and a collared shirt with the sleeves rolled. Her hair was clipped back with a pencil.

"I am," Julian said, attempting a smile that felt more like a grimace. "Sorry I'm early. The bus got in ahead of schedule and I didn't want to wander aimlessly and look suspicious."

"You'd be surprised how often that happens here." She stepped aside. "I'm Nell, I own the inn with my husband, Owen. Welcome."

❧ ❧ ❧

The inn smelled like lemon polish, lavender, and coffee. Somewhere in the back, a radio was playing something soft and jazzy. A stack of linen napkins sat folded on the entryway table beside a vase of herbs and a clipboard that said GUESTS: Please Check In! in looping handwriting.

As they walked toward the staircase, Julian caught glimpses of the front parlor—bookshelves lining one wall, two high-backed chairs angled toward a fireplace—and a sunroom full of plants and cushioned benches. A breakfast nook tucked into the far corner had a bowl of fresh apples on the table and an oversized chalkboard with a handwritten menu.

"You're on the second floor," Nell said, leading the way upstairs. "We've only got a couple guests this week—things are quieter than usual since it's the end of summer—but they'll ramp up soon as we enter September."

Julian perked up at that but didn't ask. Not yet. He had read that this was a popular town to visit in the fall.

She handed him a key with a brass tag that read Room 3.

"Let me know if you need anything," Nell said. "And feel free to poke around the house. Just don't open any cupboards marked PRIVATE unless you want to get scolded by a ghost."

Julian blinked. "The—sorry?"

"Just teasing," she winked, smiling as she turned toward the stairs. "Mostly."

❧ ❧ ❧

His room overlooked the square, and the bed had a hand-stitched quilt folded neatly at the foot. Everything was clean and slightly mismatched in the most intentional way possible—which he found quite common, and charming, in old New England inns.

He dropped his bag on the bench beneath the window and stood for a moment, soaking it in.

The floors creaked slightly underfoot, the wallpaper was faintly floral with an aged patina that felt earned rather than worn. A bookshelf held a few classic novels and a slim binder titled <u>A History of the Maplewick Inn: Collected Notes by the Guests Who Knew Her Best</u>. The binder was full of anecdotes—stories of lost rings, ghost sightings, wedding proposals, mysterious dreams. He made a mental note to read through it later.

Next to the binder sat a leather-bound book he didn't remember unpacking—its spine cracked, its edges feathered with age. When he reached for it, a single page turned on its own, stopping at a short handwritten note in looping script:

Ask her about the square.

He glanced toward the window, then back at the page. The handwriting was old-fashioned—fountain pen ink, not ballpoint. A draft lifted the corner of the paper, though the window was firmly shut.

Julian set it back on the shelf slowly.

He made a mental note to ask Nell about the book later... or maybe about the ghost cupboards.

୬ ୬ ୬

Nell was in the kitchen when he came back down, stirring something on the stove with one hand and scribbling notes on a scrap of paper with the other.

"I don't suppose there's a bookstore in walking distance?" he asked.

"There's only one," Nell said, without missing a beat. "Whitlock Books—just across the square."

"Whitlock..." Julian tilted his head. "As in one of the founding families?"

Nell's mouth quirked. "You've done your research."

"A little," he admitted. "Couldn't help it — Maplewick's history is... unusual."

"You have no idea," she said with a smile. "My cousin Mavis runs the shop. If she doesn't have the book you're looking for, it probably doesn't exist."

Julian nodded.

"Tell her I sent you," Nell added. She grinned, then waved him off. "Go. You'll like her."

❧ ❧ ❧

Julian stepped out into the morning light, his steps crunching on the path as he made his way across the square. The wind smelled faintly of bread and something herbal, and the air had that odd combination of stillness and motion he'd only ever felt in very old places.

Somewhere near the center of the square, he thought he heard a woman humming—a lilting, tuneless sound, like someone waiting for company. When he turned, no one was there. Just the breeze and the sway of a maple branch overhead.

He adjusted his bag and kept walking, but couldn't shake the feeling that the town was somehow watching him.

Chapter Three

The bell above the door didn't ring, it jingled, as it did when it was excited.

Julian stepped into Whitlock Books with a soft creak of the old floorboards and the quiet certainty that he'd already done something wrong.

The shop didn't feel like other bookshops. It felt older, quieter—not just quiet in sound, but quiet in spirit, like it was listening to him and hadn't decided yet if he belonged.

He adjusted his satchel and glanced around.

To his left, a wall of secondhand paperbacks leaned gently toward one another like old friends. To his right, a glass case held rare and antique titles, the kind he usually had to make appointments to see. Farther back, a wooden arch led to a cozier space with armchairs, a fireplace, and a long low table scattered with current bestsellers and carefully stacked bundles wrapped in twine.

The scent hit him next—paper, dust, something herbal. Like the whole shop had steeped in tea.

He took a step forward and a book fell gently off the shelf.

Julian blinked. "Uh."

He picked it up and turned it over in his hands.

That's when he noticed her.

№ № №

Mavis Whitlock stood behind the counter, half-shadowed by a shelf, a mug in one hand and a pen in the other.

She was in her early forties, he guessed, with thick, wavy, dark hair swept into a twist and a cardigan the same shade as rosewood. She wore a long skirt and flat brown boots, and there was something in the way she held her cup—like she had a hundred things to do but had promised herself she'd finish the tea first.

Her eyes were sharp and steady behind reading glasses. Her expression was calm, unreadable.

Julian tried not to look like someone who talked to books when he was alone.

"Sorry," he said, lifting the volume slightly. "This fell."

"It does that sometimes," she replied.

Her voice was low and clear, with the slightest rasp. The kind of voice that made you think of old songs or people who read aloud for a living.

"Right," he said, then cleared his throat. "I'm Julian Everett. Nell sent me. From the inn."

Something about her softened at that.

"She said you'd be by," Mavis said. She set down her mug and came out from behind the counter.

Julian's brain was trying to catalogue her: quiet, warm, probably intimidating if she wanted to be. She smelled faintly like cedar and the tea from next door.

She held out her hand for the book he was still holding.

"Let me guess," she said. "You're looking for town records, obscure local legends, and anything about that one person who maybe saw a ghost once and never stopped talking about it?"

Julian grinned, relieved. "That's alarmingly accurate."

"It's a popular combo."

She walked over to a shelf near the back, tucked between New England history and folklore. Julian followed, trying not to look too eager.

"You're working on a book?" she asked.

"A series of articles, actually. For a historical journal. I'm visiting old towns across New England—documenting their architecture, ghost stories, founding myths. That sort of thing."

Mavis nodded. "Maplewick's good for all three."

"Yeah, I'm already suspicious of how picturesque it is."

"I won't hold that against you."

She pulled down three books and handed them over—one slim, one thick, one spiral-bound with faded handwritten notes on the cover.

Julian took them reverently.

"I'll probably be in here a lot, if that's alright," he said.

Mavis raised an eyebrow. "I'm not sure you have a choice."

He looked up.

"The shop's already decided it likes you," she added.

He blinked. "Sorry?"

"Nothing," she said, turning back toward the counter. "Let me know if you need anything."

Julian watched her for half a second longer than he should have, then retreated into a chair near the fireplace and opened the thickest book in the stack.

Somewhere behind him, a floorboard creaked—and in a corner he couldn't see, Hattie hovered silently and rolled her eyes.

❧ ❧ ❧

Mavis watched Julian settle into the big navy chair by the fireplace—the one with the patched arm and the pillow no one ever moved. He angled himself so the light hit the pages just right, like someone who knew how to read in a room with lamps instead of screens.

He had kind eyes, she thought. And hair that couldn't quite decide if it was neat or messy—dark and curling a little at the edges, like it had once been combed but had since made its own decisions. His blazer was slightly rumpled in the back, and he wore the look of a man who spent more time thinking about sentences than about lunch.

The book he'd opened was an obscure local compendium—part town history, part speculation, part recipe book, oddly enough. It had been donated by a woman who swore the founder of Maplewick had kept a pet crow. Mavis wasn't entirely sure that wasn't true.

She liked watching people read. Not in a weird way—she just liked seeing the moment their shoulders dropped, when their breathing changed, when they stopped reaching for their phone and started turning pages like they'd forgotten there was anything else to do.

Julian Everett was already in that zone.

❧ ❧ ❧

The bell above the door stayed silent as Max arrived from school, cheeks pink from the walk and backpack sliding off one shoulder like it always did.

He stomped in, let the door slam a little too hard, and called, "Hi, I'm home! I'm starving!"

"You're always starving," Mavis said from the counter.

"I'm ten. It's a medical condition."

Without waiting for further discussion, he crossed into the bakery side. "Aunt Ruth! Did you save me something?"

"Behind the register, sugar bug," Ruth's voice called back. "Don't inhale it."

Max returned a moment later holding a warm scone in one hand and a tea in the other, looking supremely pleased with himself.

He took a bite, then, noticing Julian reading in the back chair, leaned toward his mom. "That guy looks like a science teacher who gets excited about moss."

"Be nice," Mavis murmured.

"I am being nice."

⁊❦ ⁊❦ ⁊❦

Julian finally looked up after what must have been twenty quiet minutes.

He blinked once, adjusted his glasses, and turned toward the counter.

"These are... incredible," he said, gesturing to the stack. "You've already saved me two weeks of work."

Mavis nodded. "We try."

He smiled, then glanced at Max. "Hey there."

"Hey," Max said through a mouthful of scone.

Julian stood and placed the books carefully on the checkout counter. "I'll be back tomorrow, if that's alright."

"You're welcome anytime," Mavis said, and meant it.

He hesitated for a moment, like he might say something else, then just nodded and left, the door closing gently behind him.

The moment he was gone, the shop seemed to exhale.

ᘐ ᘐ ᘐ

Mavis leaned against the counter and glanced at the books he'd left behind. One of them was still open, spine up—he'd tucked a small slip of paper inside as a makeshift bookmark; his handwriting was tidy and narrow.

She reached for it.

The moment her fingers touched the edge of the page, a faint thread of golden light lifted from the paper—delicate as spider silk, drifting upward like it might float away. It coiled briefly in the air before fading into nothing, leaving behind the ghost of warmth on her fingertips.

Her breath caught. She hadn't seen her magic stir like that in years.

Quietly, she closed the book, tucking the slip of paper back inside.

Behind her, a soft draft curled around her shoulders, and she felt the faintest sense of being watched.

She turned toward the far shelf.

There stood Hattie—arms loosely folded, spectacles perched on her nose, cheeks flushed with a perpetual ghostly rosiness like she was always mid-laugh.

Hattie had been part of the bookshop since its beginning and carried herself like someone who still couldn't believe her good fortune. She looked to be in her late fifties with silver curls pinned back in a twist, and today she wore a soft plum sweater over a wide, floaty skirt that shifted as if stirred by a breeze only she could feel.

To the untrained eye, the corner was empty.

To Mavis and Max, Hattie was right there—beaming, observant, and visibly delighted.

"What?" Mavis said under her breath in an annoyed tone.

Hattie's grin widened.

A book nudged itself forward on the nearest shelf.

"Hattie," Mavis warned.

Max wandered over, licking crumbs from his fingers. "Is she doing it again?"

"She's doing it again."

He looked up at Hattie and whispered, "Mom says you have to let people figure stuff out, don't be so pushy."

Hattie gave a playful little shrug and tilted her head toward the door Julian had just walked through. "He dog-ears his pages," she said, sighing like a fond aunt. "But otherwise? Promising."

Mavis rolled her eyes and tried not to smile.

Chapter Four

The Knittery smelled like wool and lemon shortbread, with a faint undercurrent of lavender. Afternoon light poured through the tall front windows, turning the glass jars of buttons into jewel-toned constellations.

Mavis slipped in through the side door, brushing cool air from her cardigan sleeves. She was late, and the circle had already begun.

Eight women sat in mismatched chairs around a large oak table, skeins of yarn pooled in their laps like bright rivers. Two of those women were not technically alive, though here in The Knittery, that was more of a footnote than a revelation.

Mavis's mother, Irene, was in her favorite wingback chair by the hearth, a long, silvery braid down her back and a scarf-in-progress stretched between her hands. She barely glanced at the yarn ball on the far counter before it slid off the stack and rolled across the floor to her feet, obedient as a cat.

Agnes, her sister, sat across from her—knitting needles hovering in midair, clicking away without her touching them, her hands free to pour tea for the others. She was laughing at something Beatrix, the ghost of their great-great-aunt, had just said. Beatrix was half-faded in the sunlight, a knitted shawl wrapped around her spectral shoulders, a basket of phantom yarn at her feet.

"About time," Agnes said when she spotted Mavis. "We were about to call for Hattie to come fetch you by the ear."

"She's busy," Mavis said, pulling off her cardigan and dropping into the empty chair between her cousin, Lydia, and a vacant one clearly meant for a ghost—its knitting project floating steadily in midair. "And I was... working."

Lydia smirked. "Is that what we're calling it now?"

Mavis gave her a flat look. "Don't start."

Beatrix's needles paused mid-row. "We hear you've had a certain historian in your shop," she said in her lilting, just-on-the-edge-of-mischief voice.

"You 'hear' everything," Mavis said, reaching for the plate of shortbread.

Irene and Agnes exchanged a glance over the top of their knitting. An amused look that said they'd already discussed something and were simply waiting for the rest of the room to catch up.

"Some of us," Agnes said mildly, "have been informed—by rather reliable sources—that he's not here by accident."

"Reliable sources meaning the ghosts," Lydia translated.

"Not all the ghosts," Beatrix said, her expression mock-offended. "Just the ones with any sense."

Mavis broke a piece of shortbread in half and tried not to roll her eyes. "I've known him for less than a day."

"That's how it starts," her mother said, pulling a length of yarn from across the room with a twitch of her fingers. It arced neatly through the air, landing in her lap without so much as a tangle.

One of the living women at the table—a lifelong Maplewick resident named Myrtle—leaned in conspiratorially. "My Eddie and I met over a spilled bag of flour. Married forty-three years."

Mavis popped the shortbread into her mouth. "This is not a spilled flour situation."

Agnes's floating needles paused just long enough for her to wink. "We'll see."

The circle rippled with chuckles and the quiet clack of knitting. A ghost at the far end of the table—a portly man in suspenders who liked to linger here on Thursdays—cleared his throat and launched into a story about the first Maplewick

Harvest Festival. The yarn in Mavis's hands wound itself neatly into a ball as she listened, and she didn't bother to stop it.

Here in The Knittery, magic happened as naturally as breathing. And sometimes, so did matchmaking.

Chapter Five

The best plans began with tea, notebooks, and at least one person in denial about how much work it would be.

The Maplewick Inn smelled like warm scones, polished wood, and a bit of pine from the branch Nell had tucked into the vase on the entry table. Mavis stepped inside and exhaled. The inn always smelled like someone had recently fluffed the pillows and lit a candle, even if no one had.

Built in 1787, the inn had seen centuries of visitors—some of whom, if the stories were to be believed, hadn't entirely left. A soft draft curled along the hallway as she passed, as if one of those unseen guests had leaned forward to peek at the paper tucked under her arm. The inn's walls held secrets and hospitality in equal measure, and everything from the creaking floorboards to the mismatched armchairs gave off the feeling that you were always welcome. Centuries old, and looked it in the best way—wide pine floors, hand-hewn beams, leaded glass windows that caught the morning sun in fractured patches of light. Nothing matched perfectly, but somehow it all belonged.

Mavis followed the sound of voices to the back parlor, where the familiar buzz of her cousins and sister let her know she was late.

ॐ ॐ ॐ

The room was warm and sunlit, scattered with clipboards,tea cups, and Lydia's coveted seasonal tea sachets, which she always brought even if no one asked. Ruth was already doodling recipes in the margins of the schedule, and Nell was rosy cheeked; she was as in her element planning a cozy retreat as an accountant was when all of their numbers added up.

"Okay," Ruth was saying as Mavis stepped into the room, "but if we do the lavender lemon scones again, we have to cut back on the glaze. That comfort recipe is strong and last time we had weepers."

"That's not a bad thing," said Lydia, smiling into her tea. "Sometimes people need to cry about scones."

Lydia was the eldest of the cousins, Nell's older sister, and had always given the impression of someone who knew where the good pens were kept. She wore her silver-streaked hair loose today, and her clothes always looked like something out of a gardener-core catalog: long linen skirts, quiet embroidery, practical aprons. She ran her apothecary out of the general store her husband's family had owned for generations.

"Ok," Ruth agreed, "and we'll also have the orange cardamom scones unless someone plans to physically stop Susan from baking, them... they're her favorite contribution because she likes watching the joy spread as people eat them."

"Oh I do love that too," Nell sighed. "Not that she would listen even if we told her not to. She pretends she's not baking and then we all 'discover' three dozen cinnamon rolls in the morning like magic elves brought them."

"That's part of why I married her," Ruth said, grinning. Then added with a wink, "not complaining." The other women nodded. Susan's cinnamon rolls were legendary in their family.

Lydia, seated cross-legged on the floral settee, sipped her tea with the patience of a woman used to waiting out storms—whether emotional, magical, or sugar-fueled. She raised one eyebrow toward Mavis in greeting. "We started without you."

"I assumed," Mavis said, dropping into her usual armchair. "Max had a sock emergency."

"He's ten," Ruth said. "They're contractually obligated to have sock issues."

Nell held up her clipboard like a precious treasure. "We're on page two of the agenda."

"I brought my notes," Mavis said, pulling out a folded piece of paper. "They're very professional."

"Ah, yes written on the back of a bakery receipt," Ruth pointed out.

"See, very business minded." Mavis winked.

⁊ ⁊ ⁊

As the conversation turned to guest lists, Lydia glanced down at her intake sheet. "Looks like we've got a few big transitions this time. One guest wrote: 'I'm middle-aged and don't know how I got here so fast, I feel lost.'"

There was a pause, but it wasn't heavy. Just respectful. Familiar.

"Sounds like last Tuesday," Ruth said gently.

"I feel that in my joints," Nell added.

"And in my pantry," said Lydia. "I impulse-bought seven kinds of herbal tea this week."

"They'll fit in the welcome kits," Mavis offered.

Lydia grinned. "They were always going to."

"Planning these weekends always reminds me of how much they matter," Nell said after the group had discussed the rest of the guest's entries. "Even when we don't know exactly what someone needs, they always end up finding it."

"Or Hattie does," Mavis said.

Ruth nodded. "She's got a gift. Last time she found that woman a book about making peace with small regrets, and the woman burst into tears."

"She also gave someone a memoir about hiking the Appalachian Trail," Mavis added.

"She'd never hiked in her life," Ruth said.

"She signed up for a walking group the next day, and that spring she met her now husband. They sent their most recent Christmas card this past season, they had just welcomed their second baby."

Lydia raised her mug. "To ghost-guided bibliotherapy."

They all clinked mugs in mock-seriousness, and the air in the room settled again—warm and humming with good work ahead. From the far bookshelf, a single volume tipped forward, then eased itself back in place, as if seconding the toast.

They spent the next hour assigning roles—Mavis on book bundles, Ruth on breakfast and desserts (with heavy support from Susan), Lydia handling welcome apothecary kits, and Nell coordinating arrivals and activities.

"I already checked the forecast," Nell said. "We've got sunshine, a couple of cozy gray mornings, and maybe a thunderstorm on the last night if we're lucky."

"Ooh," Ruth said. "Nothing like emotional breakthroughs in the rain."

"We should add tissues to the apothecary kits," Nell said.

"Already done," said Lydia.

They were winding down when the parlor door opened and Julian stepped in, holding a coffee mug and his ever-present notebook.

"So sorry," he blundered. "Nell said I could write in the front room. I didn't mean to interrupt."

"You're not!" Nell piped up, warmly. "We were just wrapping up, come on in."

Julian glanced around, then spotted Mavis. "Hi."

"Hi," she said, keeping her tone casual even as her cousins' collective interest spiked like a thermometer in the sun.

He hesitated, gave her a small smile, and then moved to the armchair nearest the fireplace. The light hit his hair as he walked, and Mavis caught herself watching a beat too long.

Ruth, of course, noticed.

"New historian in town, huh?" she said under her breath.

Mavis didn't respond.

"He's very... bookish," Lydia added helpfully.

"I'll tell Susan to make extra cookies," Ruth said.

Nell just sipped her tea and smiled into her mug.

The moment he was seated, Ruth leaned in and whispered, "Well, he's cute."

"You're married," Mavis said.

"Not to him," Ruth said cheerfully.

"I like his boots," Lydia offered. "He looks like the kind of guy who knows what year his house was built."

"He probably handwrites letters," Nell added.

"I bet he puts his name in his books," Ruth said.

"And organizes them by obscure emotional categories," Lydia said.

"He is literally sitting ten feet away," Mavis muttered, pressing her fingers to her temple.

"And reading like he doesn't hear any of us," Ruth grinned. "Which makes him even more attractive."

ッ ッ ッ

By the time they left, the retreat to-do list was longer, the tea selection had tripled, and Lydia had promised to include something courage-inducing in Mavis's own welcome kit "just in case."

Mavis lingered behind, pretending to rewrite her notes as Julian scribbled away, his brow furrowed in concentration. He looked like someone who had a very full mind and didn't quite know what to do with all of it. It was... endearing.

Mavis smiled to herself.

She folded her notes, stood, and slipped quietly out the front door, the scent of herbs and baking and woodsmoke in the air as she stepped into the sunlit square. Behind her, the inn gave a long, contented sigh in its beams, like a house pleased with the shape of the day.

Chapter Six

Maplewick's village square was the kind of place that made people believe in storybook towns. Stone paths curved gently around garden beds still bright with late-summer blooms, and the window boxes along the shops spilled over with trailing nasturtiums and faded blue lobelia. A hand-painted sign outside Hearth & Bloom promised fresh dahlias and "possibly too much ribbon," and someone had propped a tiny broom against the door of the general store as if it might sweep the stoop itself, which it probably would.

Mavis crossed the square with her tote bag swinging at her hip, her breath catching faintly in the way it always did when the sunlight hit the weathered shingles of the bookshop just right. The Whitlock Bookshop had stood on the corner for generations, its crooked windows and slate-blue trim welcoming readers like old friends. The bell above the door gave a soft chime—not quite a ring, more a note of greeting—as she stepped inside.

"Afternoon," came Hattie's voice from somewhere near the poetry shelves. "You've got a boy upstairs who's eaten half the strawberries out of the fridge and left the green tops in a trail like a storybook breadcrumb path."

Mavis smiled. "At least he's eating fruit."

"Oh, he's healthy as a horse. Just untidy as a raccoon with a lockpick."

There was a soft rustle—papers shifting, maybe, or a chair nudging back into place. Hattie was always tidying, even if no one saw her do it.

The shop was warm and dusky with the faint scent of tea, lemon wood polish, and old paper. A customer had left a tea mug balanced atop a stack of cookbooks—Ruth or Susan would be in soon to take it back to the bakery.

Mavis headed upstairs.

Her apartment always smelled soothing—lavender, lemon, and a hint of peppermint; a blend that Lydia had given her for the diffuser she kept near the bookshelf. The soft scent always greeted her like an exhale, grounding her as much as the warm light from the windows or the stack of half-read books on the side table.

From the kitchen, she heard the gentle hum of Max's voice. He was perched at the table with a bowl of granola and a comic book open beside him, legs swinging and socked feet mismatched as usual.

"Hey, buddy," she said, setting her tote by the door.

He grinned mid-chew. "Hey. Guess what?"

"What?"

"We talked about the Autumn Festival in class today. Mrs. Walsh said our class gets to run a booth again this year and we'll have to sign up for shifts."

"Oh, that'll be fun. Do you know what kind of booth yet?"

"Nope, but I hope it's something cool. Not like the popcorn one from last year that made my clothes smell like burnt socks." He wrinkled his nose.

"I do remember that," Mavis said, smiling as she cracked open a window. The breeze that swept in carried the faintest scent of cinnamon and chimney smoke—Maplewick's early hints of fall.

Max spooned another bite into his mouth, "I hope this year we can do a candy corn booth." He said with a full mouth—then added, after swallowing, "Aunt Susan said I should go back down to the bakery and get Ivy and Benji before I start homework."

Mavis raised an eyebrow. "And yet..."

"Hattie said I could come up for a snack if I left the door open so she could hear me call if I needed anything," he said, pointing to the apartment door still ajar.

From downstairs, the faint chime of the shop bell sounded—one clear note, though no one had entered. Hattie's way of signaling the affirmative to Mavis.

"Well negotiated," Mavis said, kissing the top of his head as she passed. "Don't forget to rinse your bowl."

Max groaned with theatrical drama but obeyed. "So many rules in this house."

"Ugh, such a hard life, being responsible," she replied.

Mavis smiled to herself. The bookshop had been closed during the planning meeting, and Hattie had spent the quiet hour tidying shelves, fluffing cushions, and, no doubt, judging the crooked placement of the poetry display.

Mavis poured herself a cup of tea and settled near the window, notebook in her lap. A dozen things waited to be done: book bundles to curate, welcome letters to write, and candy corn booth ideas to help Max brainstorm. But she didn't move just yet.

Outside, the sky was softening to gold. The square was quiet. Somewhere, the old church bell chimed the hour—its mellow tone folding into the town like a lullaby.

And below, through the warped old glass, Mavis saw Julian cross the square, notebook under his arm, head tilted slightly as if cataloging the town in his mind.

She stood still watching him for a moment.

From behind her, Max's voice piped up.

"So... do you *like* him like him?"

Mavis blinked, startled. "What?"

"You're staring," Max said through a mouthful of granola. "It's like when Hattie finishes rearranging the poetry section. Intense, but happy."

Mavis gave him a look. "You know, in some cultures it's illegal for ten-year-olds to be that observant."

He grinned. "It's okay if you do. Like him, I mean."

She raised an eyebrow. "Oh, is it?"

"Yeah," he said, very seriously. "I mean, he has to like books and snacks. That's non-negotiable."

Mavis smiled, her heart giving a small, surprised ache. "Duly noted."

Max got up from the table and grabbed his empty bowl. "I'll go get Ivy and Benji. We'll meet you at the table downstairs."

"Don't forget to rinse it," she called to his back.

"I never forget," he yelled dramatically from the sink.

She waited until she heard the shop door shut behind him at the bottom of the stairs before sitting back down. Her tea had gone lukewarm. Outside, Julian had already disappeared around the corner.

Mavis hadn't dated anyone—not really—since Max was born. She'd gone on a few dates over the past year, but before that there'd been no time, no space, and honestly, it hadn't felt like it was worth the effort.

But now... Max was getting older and more independent and Mavis felt her heart being ready for something new. She had long been over the handsome, charismatic guest who had passed through eleven years ago and wrapped her into a whirlwind romance. She had loved him for a moment and from that love, she got Max; her greatest treasure. She hadn't known his father would leave as quietly as he came so she hadn't thought of anything but mending her heart when he left without a goodbye. In the months that followed her family had gathered around her and helped heal her broken heart, and by the time she realized she was pregnant with Max, his father was long gone. He had never returned. Maplewick loved Max, he was a favorite child of many; and he was a cherished part of the Whitlock family. Mavis carefully answered every question of Max's, and was prepared for the feelings that might come, but so far Max seemed to feel loved and secure. Not having a dad was as normal for him as having one was for some others.

Mavis's thoughts turned to Julian. She wasn't interested in rushing anything. She was just... noticing.

She lifted her mug again, and for a fleeting second the curl of steam rose in the shape of a heart. Mavis made a wry face at it before it vanished into the air.

Chapter Seven

The bell above the shop door gave a soft chime. Not the stranger's chime, but the kind that meant someone good is here.

Julian stepped into the bookshop, notebook under his arm and a slight flush on his cheeks from the walk across the square. He paused just inside, breathing in the warm scent of old books and something faintly citrusy—like lemon balm and tea.

Mavis looked up from the counter and tried not to smile too obviously. "Afternoon."

"Hi," Julian said. "I hope it's okay I came by—I was going to write at the inn, but someone's having an extremely loud phone call about a lost sweater."

"Scandalous," Mavis said. "What color?"

"Chartreuse, apparently. I didn't know people actually wore chartreuse outside of mystery novels."

Mavis laughed. "You'd be surprised what gets left behind in Maplewick. Once someone forgot a full cello in the town gazebo. We don't even have an orchestra."

Julian grinned, then held up his notebook. "I was hoping to get some writing done. Would it be alright if I used the table near the window?"

"It's a good table," she said. "Quiet. Has opinions about ink color, but otherwise friendly."

Julian blinked, then gave a small, amused shake of his head. "This shop really does have a personality."

She tilted her head, eyes gleaming, and smiled at him.

He made his way over and set his things down. Mavis followed, pretending to straighten a pile of returned books on a nearby shelf.

"What are you working on?" she asked.

"Article series," he said. "I'm visiting a dozen historical towns in New England, writing essays about their hidden histories. I was going to start in Portsmouth, but something about Maplewick drew me in. I'm already behind on my outline, but I'm not sorry."

"Hidden histories are our specialty," Mavis said. "If you're interested, I could show you the family archives sometime. Or the old cemetery, if you're into dramatic epitaphs and leaning headstones."

Julian looked up at her, that same thoughtful expression in his eyes. "I'd love that."

Mavis tucked a piece of hair behind her ear. "Then I'll take you."

Before either of them could say more, the half-door to the bakery flew open, and Max burst in from the other side.

"I got Ivy and Benji!" he announced. "They were finishing cookies."

"I was inspecting the raisins," Benji added solemnly.

"Did they pass?" Julian asked.

"Mostly," Benji said. "But one was suspicious."

Ivy rolled her eyes and dropped her backpack at the homework table. "He licked it and put it back."

"I did not!" Benji squeaked.

Mavis pointed a gentle finger. "Homework first, then more cookies. And no licking the supplies."

"We're doing spelling," Max said to Julian. "Very serious. I have 'autumn' and 'festival.' Ivy has 'pumpkin' and 'October.'"

Benji piped up, "I have to write my name and draw something that starts with B."

Julian smiled. "What did you pick?"

"A bear on a bicycle."

"Ambitious," Mavis said. "Classic 'B' behavior."

The front bell chimed again, and this time it was the fuller kind of arrival: her mother, Irene Whitlock, and Aunt Agnes bustled in, both smelling faintly of wool scarves and warmth.

"Look at all my favorite people," Irene said brightly. She unwound her scarf, gave it a brisk shake, and the lingering raindrops vanished in a shimmer of air, leaving the fabric crisp and dry.

Agnes set a small muslin pouch on the counter. "I brought lemon balm from the garden." The moment the bundle touched the wood, the scent unfurled in a wave so vivid it seemed to curl through the whole room, sweeter and sharper than herbs had any right to be.

Julian's pen stilled halfway across the page. He glanced around, as if expecting someone else to react—but everyone carried on without pause. He shook his head faintly, lips quirking in a private, uncertain smile.

"And I brought backup," Irene added, producing a tin of cookies from her oversized bag.

Susan was behind her, holding a fresh teapot. "And I brought tea, because I know how this goes."

Ruth came through the connecting archway, brushing flour off her hands. "And I brought myself."

The kids barely looked up as tea was poured and cookies were passed around. Agnes complimented Ivy's penmanship. Irene asked Max if his teacher still used the squeaky whiteboard. Benji requested a cookie that "didn't have yucky raisins that looked like poop in them."

"That's a valid stance," Julian said, glancing up from his notebook.

"Thank you," Benji replied with deep sincerity.

Mavis drifted back behind the counter, letting the sounds of family and warmth fill the shop.

Julian looked up from his notes, smiling softly. "Your family's kind of incredible," he said.

Mavis shrugged, pretending not to be flustered. "They're very fond of snacks and showing up unannounced."

"Sounds kind of nice." He said softly.

For a long moment, they just looked at each other, and something warm moved between them. Quiet, but real.

Julian stood politely as the room filled.

"Mavis," Irene said, turning to him. "Aren't you going to introduce us?"

"Oh—sorry," Mavis said. "Everyone, this is Julian Hart. He's a historian, here writing about small towns like ours."

Julian offered a hand. "Nice to meet you."

"Irene Greymoor-Whitlock," Mavis's mom said, shaking it. "And this is my sister, Agnes Greymoore-Fenwick; Nell and Lydia's mother. She used to run the inn, back before Nell took over."

"I'm staying there now," Julian said. "It's... lovely. Historic and homey all at once."

Agnes beamed. "It's been in our family for generations. I'm so glad you're enjoying it."

"I'm writing about lesser-known histories," Julian explained. "Places with heart. And age. And stories. And Greymoor... another founding family, right?"

"Well done," Irene said. "And you came to the right town. My husband and I used to run this bookshop and the bakery next door before we passed them on to our daughters. Maplewick's full of stories, and Mavis is the one to ask if you want the real ones—not just what's on the plaques."

Julian turned to Mavis, visibly intrigued. "Is that right?"

"She knows everything," Ruth said helpfully. "Especially the weird stuff."

"Thanks," Mavis said dryly.

Julian smiled at her. "I'd love a tour sometime. If you're willing."

She hesitated, then nodded. "Sure. Let's start with the cemetery. The old part—no plaques, lots of stories."

"Tomorrow?"

"I'll meet you after breakfast," she said. "Don't forget your boots. Some of the ghosts are picky about footwear."

Julian blinked. "Wait, was that a joke?"

Mavis just grinned and walked away.

The rest of the hour passed in a hum of spelling words, cookies, and soft conversations. Benji showed off his bear drawing. Ivy and Max argued (mildly) about the spelling of lantern. The adults shared tea and murmured gossip and occasionally called out encouragement from across the room.

And at the corner table, Julian sat quietly, watching, writing, smiling like someone who had found something he hadn't realized he was looking for.

In the back room, a chair gave a soft, distinct creak, as though someone had just settled into it. A moment later, a book spine slid flush against its neighbors on the shelf, though no one was near enough to touch it.

Mavis didn't turn—she didn't have to. She knew Hattie had decided this was worth watching.

Chapter Eight

The next afternoon, by three-fifteen, Whitlock Books had settled into that after-school hush where pencils scratch, chairs scoot, and someone always asks if a cookie counts as "brain fuel." Mavis had spread the big checked cloth across the homework table and set down a chipped crock of pencils, a jar of erasers, and three mugs of mint tea that Ruth had labeled MAX, IVY, and BENJI with a wax pencil like they were dignitaries.

Max and Ivy were bent over spelling lists—lantern, harvest, festival—while Benji drew an increasingly fierce bear riding an increasingly complicated bicycle. A narrow sunbeam fell across the table like a bookmark.

"Okay," Mavis said, tapping the page with a friendly pen. "Ten more good minutes, then cookies." She took inventory of what was happening with their work. "Nice, Benji—I like that your bear is wearing its helmet."

Benji's tongue poked out in concentration. "It's safety."

"Exactly."

A small draft lifted the corner of Ivy's worksheet. It wasn't the window. The window was closed.

"Afternoon, Aunt Bea," Max said without looking up.

Mavis glanced toward the end of the table and smiled at the empty chair there. Empty to most people. To Maplewickians, it held a spry woman in her late seventies with glossy hair wound into a no-nonsense bun, eyes that missed nothing, and a sweater the color of a storm cloud. Beatrix—spinster aunt, patron saint of neat margins, and the graveyard's most dedicated truant— folded herself into place like she'd never left.

"Afternoon, ducks," Beatrix said, her voice brisk and warm. "Let's not confuse lantern with latern, hmm? Two Ns, two consonants holding hands."

Ivy corrected the word before Mavis could say a thing. Her pencil ticked a tidy n into the right place. "Thanks, Aunt Bea."

Benji held up a sheet of stickers. "Do you want a hedgehog?"

"Tempting," Beatrix said, amused. "But no. I'm not a hedgehog person. Put him on your helmeted bear; he looks like he needs a friend."

The bell above the front door gave a gentle someone-good-is-here chime. Julian stepped in, shoulder bag slung crosswise, hair ruffled from the breeze signaling September's arrival. He paused at the threshold, then remembered he was holding a paper sack.

"Pastry delivery," he said, lifting it a little. "Nell caught me on my way out of the inn and decided I looked responsible enough to carry scones across town."

"Questionable judgment," Mavis teased, though her smile gave her away.

He set the bag on the table by the window and leaned on the table's edge. "What's everyone working on?"

"Spelling," Ivy said.

"Art," Benji said, as if that explained both the bear and the helmet's racing stripes.

"Not panicking," Max said solemnly. "And festival. Which has a sneaky 'a' that sounds like a 'u'."

"Treacherous," Julian agreed.

Mavis poured him a mug of tea before he could refuse. "Staying?"

"Not this time," he said with a rueful little smile. "I need a quiet spot before my brain gets stolen by, uh—" he gestured toward Benji's bear "—whatever that is."

"It's safety," Benji said again, deadpan.

Julian chuckled. "Of course it is. Well... enjoy the scones."
He gave them all a quick nod and slipped back out. The bell
chimed once in approval, then stilled.

Only when the door shut did Beatrix slide a small, old-
fashioned ruler toward Max. It skated across the wood grain
with exaggerated propriety and stopped at his elbow. Max
picked it up without looking, like this happened every day.

"Form," Beatrix said briskly. "Letters sit on the line, not in a
hammock above it."

The erasers in the jar rearranged themselves into tidy pairs,
like ballroom dancers finding partners. Ivy's pencil rolled back
to her hand. A dictionary eased itself open to harvest with a
gentle sigh.

Max straightened. "Yes, ma'am."

"Benji," Beatrix continued, swiveling with an elegance that
had nothing to do with gravity. "If your bear is on a bicycle, his
knees must bend. Otherwise he'll crack like a wishbone."

Benji obligingly added knees. "What's a wishbone?"

"Something you regret breaking if you're superstitious,"
Beatrix said, and then softened at his frown. "It's just a bone.
Draw your knees."

Mavis pretended to sort a stack of returns but really watched them all with her cheek in her hand, soft and full. This—this ordinary table with its extraordinary company—was her favorite kind of magic.

Ruth slipped in through the bakery door with the stealth of a woman who knew how to interrupt without interrupting. She slid a plate of shortbread onto the table, kissed the tops of three heads, and squeezed Mavis's shoulder on her way out. "Tea top-up in five," she whispered. "Don't let Susan see Benji beg for two cookies. She's soft."

"I heard that," Susan called from the kitchen, clearly not that far away.

Beatrix shook a page straight with one quick flick of her fingers. "Ivy, darling, your October needs a capital. It's a proper name for a proper month."

Ivy capitalized obediently. "There," she said, pleased.

"Alright," Mavis said, clapping once, gently. "Ten minutes done. Cookies, then round two." She slid the bag to Max to be distributor. "And someone thank your honorary tutor for her service."

"Thank you, Aunt Bea," came a three-child chorus.

Beatrix preened. "My pleasure. I accept payment in Latin roots and occasional gossip."

Benji broke his shortbread in half. "What's your rate?"

"For gossip?" she asked. "Dangerous question."

He giggled, and shoved the other half of the shortbread into his mouth. For few minutes there were sounds of giggling and cookie eating as the children took a short break.

"Alright, teams," Beatrix said, brisk again. "Ivy, trade with Max—his harvest needs a neat-checker; yours could use a second pair of eyes on festival. Benji, I expect you to give that bear a bell."

"A bell?" Benji lit up. "Can it be blue?"

"Any bell brave enough to ring can be any color it likes," Beatrix decreed.

Another dictionary—one of the fat ones with onion-skin pages—slid half an inch farther out of the shelf and opened itself to 'festival' with a gentle little sigh. Max blinked at it, then leaned in. "Show-off," he murmured fondly.

Beatrix made her way over to Mavis, smoothing the air above a stack of worksheets that obediently squared themselves. "That man," she said, glancing toward the door Julian had gone through, "did you see the way he noticed the children? He gave each of them exactly what they needed without even trying."

"Yes, he's polite," Mavis said, though her smile betrayed her.

59

Beatrix looked at her as if weighing a student. "Polite is manners. Observant is care. Trust me, I know about things." She waggled her eyebrows like a conspirator and made the teeniest shooing motion at Mavis's heart, as if to say: Go on. Don't be shy of nice things.

Mavis busied herself with stacking finished pages. "Max, this is good work," she said, voice a little warmer than before. "Ivy, your capitals are perfect. Benji—" She paused, because the bear now had a blue bell and a helmet sticker and, inexplicably, decent knees. "—this bear could win a race."

"Safety first," Benji said, and ate his cookie like a man who had earned it.

The door chime gave a small breath of sound—someone good again—and Nell poked her head in, cheeks pink from the walk. "Anyone seen Owen's measuring tape?" she asked.

"It's in your pocket," three adult women and one ghost said at once.

Nell checked, laughed, and saluted them with it. "Carry on."

Homework resumed. Pencils made their agreeable sounds. The light shifted toward honey as the square moved slowly toward evening.

When the lists were finished and the bear had won its imaginary race, the children packed their bags in the incremental, messy way of people who live in a town that never rushes anyone out the door. Ruth beckoned her children over from the bakery. Susan appeared with apples because Susan didn't believe in letting anyone do anything un-snacked. Goodbye kisses were administered. The storm-cloud sweater at the end of the table smoothed itself without hands, as Beatrix stood.

"Same time tomorrow?" Max asked.

"If your mother allows it," Beatrix said, approval in the tilt of her chin.

"We'll see," Mavis said, which everyone knew meant yes.

The kids thundered out toward the bakery, the bell obligingly quiet for three known souls. The shop, abruptly bigger without them, inhaled. "Be right back!" Max called to his mom over his shoulder.

Just before the door could shut, Julian stepped through it, as though he had been waiting just on the other side. He stepped in laughing and shaking his head merrily. "I'm... not sure what you all do differently here," he said, eyes kind, bemused, alive with it. "But I like it."

"Good," Mavis said. "So do we."

He walked to the table by the window, grabbing a pen that had been sitting there. "My favorite pen, I set it down earlier when handing over scones," he held it up as if to prove he came back for a reason other than Mavis. He gathered his things, hesitant to leave. "I'll be back after supper," he said. "If you're open."

"We're open," Mavis said. "And if we're not, the door will tell you."

He paused, as if trying to decide whether that was a joke. "Of course it will." He lifted a hand in a small wave to the general room. "Thank you."

"Anytime," Mavis said, biting back a smile.

The door closed behind him with a polite click. The bell, because it approved, gave a single contented note.

Beatrix drifted closer, skirts stirring a little wind that didn't exist. "Kind eyes," she said, like a verdict. "Nice smile. The children like him."

Mavis let out a breath she hadn't realized she'd been holding. "I noticed."

"Mm." Beatrix looked toward the window, where the square was turning the color of tea. "Let yourself enjoy his attention, dearest" she said, as if suggesting better posture. "And teach Max three Latin roots this week. He's ready."

"Bossy," Mavis said, fondly.

"Efficient," Beatrix corrected, and then, with the faintest wink, took two steps towards the door and vanished before she even got past the front counter.

Chapter Nine

The first leaves had started to change, just at the edges—and the morning air signaled that the calendar would soon officially mark the first day of fall.

Mavis met Julian outside the bookshop just after breakfast. He was standing near the lamppost, notebook tucked into the crook of his arm, wearing a soft brown sweater and well-worn boots that looked appropriately scuffed for a cemetery visit.

"Morning," she said, holding two paper cups from Ruth's bakery. "I brought tea."

"You read my mind," he said, taking the offered cup. "You didn't happen to bring a cinnamon bun too, did you?"

"Just the tea," she said, grinning. "You'll have to earn your bun."

"I'll walk respectfully and nod at gravestones."

"Then you're halfway there."

The graveyard lay just past the edge of town, behind an old stone church that looked like it had been built with stories instead of bricks. The cemetery gate creaked open ahead of them. Past the first row of stones, the trees thickened slightly, their branches crisscrossing in leafy arches. It was quiet, and pleasant. The air smelled of lichen and damp earth. The path curved through low moss-covered headstones and small family plots tucked beneath maples and evergreens.

They walked in silence for a few minutes, the crunch of gravel underfoot and the occasional call of a blue jay the only sounds. It wasn't a spooky place—it felt tended, remembered. The kind of cemetery where people still visited and left flowers, or tucked notes into the crumbling crevices of certain stones.

"Maplewick's been here longer than most towns like it," Mavis said. "English settlers arrived in the early 1700s as Europeans started moving away from the Bay. It was officially incorporated in 1759. This cemetery was added as soon as the first of the settlers died, while the church was being built."

Julian made notes as Mavis talked. "I've been meaning to tell you," Julian said after a moment, "there was a book on the table in my room when I checked into the inn. Looked ancient— leatherbound, handwritten entries, no clear title. But it's... extraordinary."

Mavis kept her face neutral, though her fingertips tingled. A faint thread-light curled between them, as if her body recognized the mention before her mind caught up. She shoved her hands quickly into her coat pockets before Julian could notice. "Extraordinary how?"

"The level of detail," he said. "Whoever wrote it had access to primary sources, diaries, family records—stuff historians can only dream about. And the entries go all the way up to... well, basically now."

"How far back does it go?"

"Early 1700s. I read about the fire in 1820 that wiped out half the town, and there's even a first-hand account of the storm that nearly took down the church bell tower in 1892."

Mavis smiled slightly. "That bell still rings."

Julian nodded, thoughtful. "It's like someone's been updating it through every generation — because the handwriting... it shifts subtly. Same style, different hands."

"I'd love to see it," Mavis said casually.

He looked at her, intrigued. "I'd be honored to get your take. You clearly know the town better than most."

They passed the old church then—stone walls dappled in morning light, stained-glass windows catching every beam. It stood tall and weathered, but steady.

"This is one of the buildings that survived both the fire and the storm," Mavis said. "So did the bookshop, the inn, and the bakery among a few other places. Although the bookshop used to be part printing press back then. It's one of the oldest bookshops in the country, as I'm sure you know." She paused before adding, "they say the town kept what it couldn't bear to lose."

Julian looked up at the steeple, then back at her. "It's like the place has a will of its own."

She didn't answer, but her smile deepened.

Julian took out his notebook. "You know all the good stuff."

"I told you—I'm an excellent guide." She winked.

They paused beside an iron bench under a sugar maple just starting to blush red. Julian glanced at the nearest gravestone— small, rounded, nearly worn smooth.

"Some of these are barely legible."

"That one belongs to Eliza Whitlock," Mavis said. "Midwife. Helped deliver over 300 babies in her lifetime, including one during a snowstorm while the house was on fire."

Julian blinked. "Seriously?"

"She wrapped the baby in her coat and helped the mother walk a mile barefoot to the next cabin. Saved them both. The house didn't make it."

He scribbled furiously. "That's incredible. How do you know all this?"

Mavis shrugged. "Family stories. My dad used to tell them over breakfast like they were fairy tales. Except they were all true."

"I love that," Julian said. "Most people forget history is personal. It's not just what's in museums—it's quilts, and recipes, and graveyards."

She glanced over at him, surprised. "Yes. Exactly that. Many families here go way back—including ours—so it really is personal."

Their eyes met for a second longer than necessary. Julian looked down, pretending to check his notes.

A breeze lifted the leaves, rustling them like old pages.

They continued walking, stopping here and there so Mavis could point out the headstones of ancestors, townspeople, and one large memorial to a cow who had saved a barn full of people during a lightning storm.

Julian took a photo of that one.

As they walked, Mavis pointed out names and stories—Nathaniel Cobb, who once tried to start a pigeon post and gave up after a single letter was returned unopened; Maybelle Hines, who had run the library out of her home until the current building was finished...

Julian took notes constantly. But he wasn't just writing—he was listening.

They came to a shaded corner where older stones leaned gently toward one another. Mavis stopped beside a tall, vine-framed headstone.

"Here they are," she said.

Julian read the inscription aloud:

Sybil Greymoor, 1728–1798. And Roland Greymoor, 1726–1797. Still arguing. Still in love.

Julian laughed. "That's... honest."

"They were a force," Mavis said. "She ran the inn for years. He ran the town council. Apparently every major decision required three arguments, one apology, and a shared slice of pie."

"It sounds like you're very familiar," Julian murmured, scribbling. "Were they yours?"

"Great-great-great-great-great-great aunt and uncle, give or take. On my mother's side. My mother and Aunt Agnes are Greymoors. Back before they were married they were called the Greymoor Girls."

He knelt for a closer look. As he did, the leaves overhead stirred sharply, though the air was otherwise still. A faint ripple of sound drifted through—half-argument, half-laughter—so soft it could be mistaken for the wind. Julian paused, frowning slightly, then shook his head and bent back to his notes.

But Mavis knew better. The Greymoors hadn't stopped bickering just because they'd been buried. She smiled faintly, not saying a word.

ɝ ɝ ɝ

They started back toward town at an easy pace, heading down the curved path that led toward the old church. The town around them felt quiet in a familiar, comfortable way—like it was pausing to let them pass.

"So what about you?" Julian asked. "You always wanted to stay in Maplewick?"

She nodded. "I thought about leaving once. But I realized I didn't want to go—I just wanted my life to feel like mine."

"And now?"

"Oh now I think I'm old enough to know that part of making your own life is being bolstered by those who love you best."

They reached the church steps. The door creaked gently in the wind, though the air was still.

Julian looked at her, a thoughtful crease between his brows. "You ever feel like this town is... I don't know... aware of you?"

Mavis smiled. "I think it's aware of everyone."

Julian cleared his throat. "So... what would you think about helping me explore more of Maplewick? I mean, if you're not tired of talking to a nerd with a notebook."

"I'd be happy to," Mavis said, surprising herself with how much she meant it. "There's plenty left to see. We could start with the archives. Or the old mill. Or the town ledger. Or..."

"Or?" he prompted.

"Or the unofficial tour. The places the town doesn't put in brochures but can't help showing you anyway."

Julian smiled. "Those are always the best places."

"You should really stay for the Autumn Festival to get a good slice-of-life." She invited hopefully.

They paused beneath a sugar maple just turning amber at the tips, its wide branches arching overhead like a canopy. Mavis leaned against the low stone wall that edged the path. Julian tucked his notebook away and took a slow breath, as if he hadn't realized he'd needed the walk until it was over.

He glanced around—at the tidy picket fences, the distant clang of a shop bell, the way sunlight filtered through the trees in golden threads. Maplewick had a way of inviting confession without asking for it.

"I should tell you something," Julian said suddenly.

Mavis looked over, curious.

"When I took the assignment to write about old New England towns, it wasn't just about the history," he said. "I mean—it was. It is. I love this stuff. But also… I was looking for something more personal."

He ran a hand through his hair, thoughtful. "For the past twenty years, I've been all over. PhD in Boston, postdoc abroad. Guest lecturing here and there. I'd spend six months in a university town, then move on. I never really stopped long enough to figure out where I wanted to be. And now I'm forty-five and I'm tired of temporary."

Mavis's expression softened. She didn't interrupt.

"I'm forty-five," Julian went on. "And I've never had a home I stayed in. I've lived in apartments with boxes I never unpacked. I kept telling myself the next town would be the one. I'm not even sure what I'm looking for exactly," he continued. "I just know I want a town with a sense of story. A place where I can live, not just work. Where I can stay."

He smiled. They stood there for a moment, the quiet between them not awkward but shared—like a bench between two friends.

He glanced at her, a little shyly now. "When the magazine offered me this series, I said yes because I wanted to find a place that felt like... home. I didn't tell anyone that part. I just said yes."

"And now?" she asked, voice quieter.

"Maplewick is the first town that hasn't felt like a stop along the way," he said. "It feels... settled. Lived in. Layered. Like I could belong here, if it let me."

He smiled softly, then added, "And the bookstore doesn't hurt."

Mavis gave a quiet laugh, the corners of her mouth turning up.

"I think," she said eventually, "Maplewick knows when someone belongs. It has a way of drawing people in when they're needed."

He glanced at her. "And do you think I'm needed?"

"I think time will tell," she said with a smile. "But you're certainly earning points."

"Oh?"

"For one, you made it through a cemetery walk without spouting any ghost puns."

"I have incredible restraint."

"And for two," she added, "you asked good questions. The town likes that."

Finally, Mavis pushed off from the wall and glanced toward the town square before she started walking, Julian matching her stride.

They'd reached the corner now. Just ahead, Ruth's bakery glowed warm in the afternoon light. The scent of cinnamon and brown sugar drifted toward them like an invitation.

Mavis gestured toward the door. "You know, I think you've earned that cinnamon bun."

Julian feigned deep thought. "Was that before or after I impressed you with my deep love of local history?"

"Oh, definitely after," she teased.

They continued walking back toward the bakery, their steps easy and unhurried. As they rounded the corner, the bell above the bakery door jingled—a warm sound, like laughter wrapped in sugar—and the smell of cinnamon, clove, and butter wrapped around them the moment they stepped into the bakery. Ruth stood behind the counter, sleeves rolled, cheeks pink with heat, and a smudge of flour on her forehead. She slid a tray of maple scones into the case without looking up.

"Well, if it isn't the man who survived a Maplewick cemetery stroll," she said. "Should I be concerned or impressed?"

"Hopefully impressed," Julian said, glancing at Mavis.

"He didn't even flinch when the wind whistled through the Greymoor plot," she added, deadpan.

"Old historian trick," he said. "Keep walking and pretend you're not questioning your life choices."

Ruth gave a low whistle. "Resilient and funny. You definitely do deserve a cinnamon bun."

"I've been told having one is the only way to earn full Maplewick citizenship."

"Correct," Ruth said, grabbing two buns and handing them over on mismatched plates. "Tea's hot. Take it next door, it's quiet. But if you rearrange the display table again, Julian, I'm revoking your bun privileges." She winked merrily.

Julian raised a hand. "No design changes, I swear."

They stepped into the bookshop, the door between the two spaces clicking shut behind them. The shift in energy was immediate—quieter, softer, like stepping into a well-worn quilt. Sunlight slanted through the tall windows, catching in the motes of dust and bathing the room in amber light.

Hattie, unseen, had tidied everything. A vase of marigolds now sat on the corner of the front desk, and someone—Mavis was sure it hadn't been her—had straightened the poetry section again.

They sat at the small table near the window. Julian took a sip of tea, then tore a piece of cinnamon bun and let out a satisfied sigh. "I see why you people stay."

"We trap you with pastry," Mavis said. "It's very sinister."

He grinned, making eye contact for an extra beat. "It's working."

They stayed like that for a moment, laughter soft between them. The marigolds on the desk seemed to brighten, petals briefly pulsing like little flames. Mavis's gaze flicked toward them, catching the faint pulse, before she looked quickly back at Julian. If Hattie wanted to give her approval, she could at least do it more subtly.

Julian hadn't noticed. But Mavis did. And warmth spread through her like tea on a cold morning, the kind that lingered, the kind that stayed.

Chapter Ten

At least twice a month, once the living had left with their flowers and their feelings, the cemetery held its own staff meeting.

The sun had not quite slipped behind the beech trees when the first voice rose—half whisper, half opinion.

"I am not against historians in principle," Sybil Greymoor announced from her vine-framed stone, "but I worry about a man who has not yet learned where he wants his roots."

"Sybil," Roland's baritone rumbled from the headstone beside hers, "you said the same about the cobbler in 1799, and he ended up mending more than boots in this town."

"He undercharged," Sybil said crisply. "Which was noble and terrible accounting."

A few stones over, June—sweet as honey but patient as weather—let a smile open. "He looks at her as though she is not just pleasant company but... important. That matters far more than having roots planted already."

Beatrix, storm-cloud sweater impeccable despite the lack of shoulders, pursed her lips. "We require steadiness. Reverence is fine, but does he have the spine to stay? Our Mavis deserves someone who doesn't vanish like fog."

June volleyed back. "He listened," she said. "And the way he looked at her, it means something."

Beatrix adjusted her spectacles purely for the satisfaction of looking severe. "Listening is the minimum viable product in a man," she said. "We require retention. And preferably application with precision."

"Bea," Sybil said, "must you hire a husband like a shop clerk?"

"I am curating standards," Beatrix sniffed. "If our Mavis is going to be paid attention to," which was the closest she could concede to anything referencing romance, "she deserves a man who files his noticing properly."

The sugar maple above the Greymoor plot gave a confidential shiver—no breeze, just opinion. From near the low wall, a warm alto called, "He had kind hands." Eliza Whitlock, midwife, stepped into view with the steadying air of a woman who had been in charge of chaos since 1768. "Caught Mavis's elbow before she slipped. Didn't even flinch. Protective and capable earns my approval."

"Kind hands matter," June agreed.

Roland folded his arms, which did nothing at all to command the situation but made him feel like he was making an important point. "Door at the bookshop liked him," he said. "Opened itself the other night. And the bell showed manners."

Sybil tilted her head toward the bookshop then back to her husband. "Hmmm. The bell is a snob. If it refrained from chiming, it's only because it already put his name on the list."

"Lists are useful," Beatrix said, cheered. "Data, I can get behind that."

From a nearby stone, "If we are making a list, let the minutes reflect he respected the cow memorial. Respect for Clover speaks well of his character." This was Mr. Hampstead—former clerk, current recorder of everything that didn't need recording and several things that did. "Respect paid to bovine heroism speaks well of a man."

"Eliza?" June asked gently. "Do you recall the cow's name?"

Eliza considered. "Clover. Brave girl. Didn't panic in lightning."

"Unlike Hank," Roland muttered.

"Unlike Hank," agreed seven stones at once, which suggested community consensus.

A small black shape slipped between two grave markers and took a seat with the unassailable poise of a monarch. Nibs, the cat, curled his tail just so and blinked.

"Ah," Sybil said. "Our barometer."

Nibs yawned, revealing the tiny pink tongue of a creature who had never been wrong.

"Judgment?" Beatrix asked him.

Nibs rotated one ear toward the village, which everyone agreed was essentially a vote.

"Very scientific," Beatrix approved.

From the far side of the path, someone cleared a spectral throat. "Best endorsement going," Eliza murmured.

"Point of order," Mr. Hampstead said, because of course he did. "We have yet to address his hat situation."

"What hat situation?" Sybil demanded.

"Doesn't own one," Mr. Hampstead said, tone grave. "Autumn approaches. A man who intends to stay must reconcile himself to wool."

"Agnes will fix that in a day," Eliza said. "You know she keeps spares for emergencies and poor taste."

From behind the Greymoor stones, a faint wind shaped itself into two voices that sounded suspiciously like bickering. It was, in fact, bickering.

"You said pie was the decider," Roland muttered.

"I said pie accompanied the decider," Sybil corrected. "Decisions are made over pie because sugar makes people honest."

June lifted her hands, calming the couple with a glance. "Let's count what matters." She ticked invisible points on invisible fingers. "He came with a notebook and not a performance. He asked permission of the place without saying the words. He looked at our girl like she is not merely pleasant company but a person he respected. He did not make a ghastly joke in the old section."

"He thought one," Roland said. "I heard it form and then he put it away like a gentleman."

"That counts," June said serenely.

"Will he stay?" Sybil asked, and for the first time her voice wasn't purely theatrical; something trembled under the polish.

The cemetery held its breath, which is a feat when you've relinquished lungs.

Roland considered the steeple, the square beyond it, the way the town rustled when it chose something. "He's tired of leaving," he said simply.

June's smile was a candle lit without fuss. "And he arrived on a day that felt like a beginning."

Beatrix lifted her chin. "Draft a report for Agnes and Irene," she said to Mr. Hampstead. "Findings to include: promising subject; actively listening; decent coat; hat deficit; kind hands; door-approved."

"Add: cat-endorsed," Sybil said.

"Add: pie-compatible," Roland said.

"Add," June murmured, soft as rain, "that Mavis looked back for him twice."

Beatrix's severity cracked at the edges. "Noted."

A small, solemn boy's voice drifted into the edges of the old section—Max, somewhere on the lane with Ivy and Benji, narrating the crucial politics of a cookie split. The ghosts turned as one toward the living sound. It put a brightness in their faces that had nothing to do with sunlight.

Eliza's gaze gentled into the kind that had calmed a hundred mothers. "It isn't just Mavis we are weighing. The boy needs someone who shows up when the ladder needs holding steady. Someone who knows a promise is a spine, not decoration."

"A child deserves more than grand entrances," Beatrix said, unusually quiet. "He deserves a man who will stay to wash the cups afterward."

Roland's gaze turned toward the square, where faint laughter drifted from the bakery. "He has the look of someone who is ready to stay put," he said simply.

June stage whispered to drive the point home. "And Mavis looked back for him *twice*."

"That's the thing," Sybil admitted, softer now. "She has had to carry her heart like an open flame. Perhaps it is time someone shielded it, instead of expecting her to keep the light on her own."

"Agreed," said every Greymoor and Whitlock-adjacent stone.

Nibs stood, shook, and trotted off toward town like a punctuation mark concluding an opinion piece.

"Meeting adjourned," Beatrix said briskly. "We'll reconvene if he attempts a pun."

Sybil slid her arm through Roland's, habit old as vows. "We'll reconvene to applaud if he brings flowers."

"Or a hat," Mr. Hampstead added, never missing the opportunity.

June tipped her head toward the maple's highest leaves, which had decided, just then, to change to a flush of red. "He'll be fine," she said. "They both will."

"On what evidence?" Sybil asked, though it came out softer than she intended.

June's eyes twinkled. "On Maplewick."

The cemetery relaxed into its late-afternoon drowse. Shadows lengthened with good manners. Someone laughed from the direction of the town square. The bell in the church tower shifted on its rope, as if clearing its throat before a blessing.

And under the Greymoor maple, a single leaf let go—just one brave red slip—and coasted down to land between two stones that had argued for the better part of three centuries and always would, side by side.

Chapter Eleven

Knitting circles had their own rhythm: part pattern, part conversation, and part the kind of silence that made confessions safer than they should be.

By Thursday evening, The Knittery glowed like a hearth. Agnes had turned on every lamp—milk-glass shades over warm bulbs—and the light pooled across old pine floors and a farmhouse table scarred with more than a century of good use. Cubby walls held skeins in orderly autumnal rainbows: pumpkin, moss, river-stone, blackberry. Above the counter, a wooden swift turned lazily on its own, winding the wool into useable balls.

Irene presided near the sideboard with the kettle, decanting hot water into mismatched mugs. Lydia continually tucked lemon balm and peppermint behind the counter "for medicinal purposes," which in her taxonomy meant "for nerves and gossip." Agnes sat at the head of the table, needles clicking like a metronome rarely bothering to look at patterns anymore.

Nell was already there, waging a gentle war with a cabled scarf that insisted on twisting at the third row. Ruth, apron swapped for a cardigan, worked a crescent shawl in russet wool and a scattering of little bobbles that looked like rosehips. Two longtime town ladies—Dorothy Calloway, retired librarian, and Mae Pierce, who ran the post office—shared an end of the table, comparing ankle sock patterns like they were recipes.

"Hydrate," Irene said, passing steaming mugs as if they were assignments. "Knitting turns reckless on an empty cup."

"Knitting turns reckless around you," Agnes muttered without looking up. "You add lace to everything."

"Lace improves morale," Irene said serenely, tucking a tin of butter cookies beside the yarn bowl.

The front door chimed. Mrs. Ramsay from Branley Lane breezed in with a tote bag full of half-finished baby hats for the church sale. A minute later, Lydia popped her head around the frame from the street—hair wind-ruffled, a basket over one arm. "Salve for cracked fingers," she announced, setting little metal pots beside the cookies. "And a witch hazel spritz for temperamental gauge."

"Gauge is a moral issue," Dorothy said primly.

"Gauge is a suggestion," Mae countered. "I knit from the heart."

"Which is why your sweaters fit the cat," Dorothy returned, already smirking.

Nell snorted, then hissed as she realized she'd purled when she should've knit. "Betrayer yarn," she said at her scarf.

"Betrayed by your own hubris," Agnes chided her daughter, snipping a tail with tidy satisfaction.

Ruth leaned back, trying not to laugh. "Nell, I told you—put a lifeline in at the end of the cable section."

"Too late," Nell said, grim but resolute. "I'm committed to this disaster."

"Lifelines are for the weak," Dorothy said.

"Dorothy," Irene said, "you once tied two circulars together with twine and prayed."

"Strategic engineering," Dorothy corrected.

The room hummed with the sort of conversation that happens when hands are busy—half an ear on the world, half on the row count. Owl buttons were admired. Someone passed around a swatch in a new wool-silk blend that smelled faintly of clean hay. A reel of measuring tape skittered across the table toward Mae at exactly the moment she said, without looking up, "Has anyone got a measure handy?" As she grabbed it she said, "thanks," to no one in particular.

Near the rafters, the air shifted like a curtain lifting. June arrived first—calm as ever, lavender-scented and soft around the edges—and took an empty chair. Beatrix followed in her storm-cloud sweater, eyes keen, hair in that no-nonsense bun that managed to look smug. Sybil swept through as if she still owned every room she entered, bracelets chiming faintly with a sound that wasn't strictly auditory. Roland trailed her, broad-shouldered, squinting at a chilly corner like it owed him rent.

Everyone looked up, the way you look when a breeze becomes a presence. Dorothy lifted a hand in greeting, casual as you please. Mae slid a mug toward the chair that June liked even though June didn't need tea anymore.

"Evening, dears," June said, voice like a warmed shawl. "Don't let me interrupt."

"You couldn't if you tried," Agnes said, but her mouth tilted into a grin. "We're planning bunting."

"Red and gold," Irene said, flipping her notebook. "Maple leaves. Bells if they don't send Roland howling."

"They do," Roland said, crossing phantom arms.

Sybil patted his sleeve. "He's sensitive. It's one of his few good qualities."

Ruth reached for a cookie. "We need more yardage this year if we're doing the lantern walk again."

"We're doing the lantern walk," Agnes confirmed, scribbling on the supply sheet. "Mavis promised to check the inventory of wire handles. Nell, can the inn handle cocoa after?"

"Obviously," Nell said. "But not the tiny marshmallows. Last year the children used them as slingshot ammunition."

Irene topped off the kettle, then tilted her head toward the dark shop windows. "Mavis texted she'll be a few minutes late."

"At least she's coming," Agnes said, rearranging stitch markers—the little tin ones that looked like autumn leaves. "She's been flitting like a wren these days."

"Wrens are happy birds," June murmured.

The door cracked and a small black cat slid inside as though he'd been invited. He leapt onto the counter with a soundless thump, sat like a loaf, and fixed the room with copper eyes.

"Nibs," Irene said. "You menace, leave the wool alone."

Nibs blinked slowly and tucked his tail around his paws and squinted as if to say: Make me.

Beatrix's mouth tightened in a smile she pretended not to have. "He prefers wool with lanolin. He can smell the good stuff."

"Can't we all," Dorothy said, fond.

The bell chimed again. Two teenage girls—Emma Duarte and Tansy Wilkes—hovered at the threshold with tote bags and hopeful faces.

"Come in," Irene said. "We'll apprentice you to the Way of Gauge."

Emma gave a shy laugh. "My mom said I should learn to knit properly instead of those... loop things I do on my fingers."

"Finger knitting is a gateway craft," Agnes decreed. "Sit. Try your hands on real needles."

Tansy eyed the shelves with awe. "If I touch that blue, will it make me a better person?"

"No," Ruth said, deadpan. "But you'll look like one."

They diffused into the table's empty chairs, eyes bright, hands clumsy in that wonderful beginning way. Lydia dabbed salve on Tansy's thumbnail. "Stop chewing. You can't pick up stitches with a ragged cuticle."

"Bossy," Tansy said, but she obeyed.

"Efficient," Lydia returned, and then, without touching it, coaxed a skein to roll gently across the table toward Emma. Emma's eyes widened; she looked at the adults to see if this was surprising. It wasn't.

"Maplewick is weird," she said softly, delighted.

91

"On purpose," Agnes said.

Soon after, Sophie and Lillian, Nell's daughters, slid through the door and pulled up chairs near to Emma and Tansy.

The room settled before the door sighed open again: Mavis at last, curls wind-swept, cheeks flushed from the walk, a tote under her arm. She paused at the sight of the full, warm room— the people who were hers. "Sorry. Susan waylaid me with 'accidental' biscotti."

"Taste testing 'accidents' being her specialty," Ruth joked. "Sit."

Mavis wedged herself between Ruth and Nell, pulled out a stubborn ball of yarn, and frowned at it like it had insulted her lineage. "I swear this knots itself to impress Agnes."

"It does," Agnes said. "Because I am its better."

"Humility," Irene said, pouring her tea.

"Never heard of her," Agnes returned. She gave Mavis's yarn a stern look, and it smoothed itself out.

They knit. And talked. And planned. Mrs. Calloway wanted table skirts for the craft booths ("No bare folding legs; we are not savages.") Mae volunteered the post office scale for weighing caramel apples ("For fairness in all things."). Nell proposed large marshmallows for the cocoa at the end of the lantern walk

("With cinnamon; without debate."). Lydia offered a pop-up apothecary table with throat lozenges and hand balms ("Festival is hard on vocal cords and cuticles. I serve where I must.").

"Max's class is running a booth," Mavis said. "Shifts start next week. He's proposing 'Guess the Candy Corn.' Ivy wants lantern crafts. Benji wants to weaponize gourds."

"No trebuchets," Ruth said automatically.

"Principal Moreno will repel the siege," Dorothy said. "She has a laminated policy."

"It's canon law at the school," Mae added.

A skein slipped from the lip of a cubby, bounced once, and nestled in the exact center of the table—a sunset-red merino with a hint of gold. It landed in front of Mavis.

"That's new," she said, surprised. "We haven't stocked this line."

Agnes and Irene exchanged a look so small you had to be kin to see it.

"Consider it a... donation," Agnes said lightly.

Sybil's smile went sideways, pleased.

Roland grunted, fond against his better judgment.

Mavis stroked the skein with her thumb. The color was brave. It made her think of the Greymoor Maple that had recently this very color.

Ruth, needles flying, didn't look up when she said, "So. Gentleman historian."

"Oh my gosh," Mavis said, immediately betrayed by her own smile. "Is this how it's going to be the entire time he's here?"

"At least," Irene said comfortably. "Tell us everything and exaggerate for entertainment."

"He brought a ledger to the shop this morning," Mavis admitted. "From the inn. Who just... finds a nineteenth-century grocer's ledger in a donation box?"

"Someone the town thinks needs a nudge," June said so softly it almost wasn't sound.

Agnes's needles kept time; her eyes were on her work. "And?"

"And..." Mavis said, trying and failing to pretend this was nothing, "he asked if I'd like to walk the ridge trail tomorrow. The old mill site."

Ruth's beaming was indecent. "Earn that bun, scholar."

"Ruth," Mavis protested, but her laughter was helpless.

Beatrix watched, pleased. Then her eyes flicked to Irene, then to Agnes, and something passed between the elder women and the ghost like smoke finding the same current. Beatrix sobered; June's hands stilled. Sybil tilted her head, listening. Roland, perhaps without choosing to, stepped nearer to Agnes the way a soul loyal to this bloodline always had.

Agnes cleared her throat. "Sophie, go fetch more peppermint, please." She did not need peppermint. But Sophie read the room, the family, and the way the air can change its temperature when her grandmother means business.

"On it," Sophie said, scraping back her chair.

"Take Emma and Tansy with you," Agnes added, because the fewer ears, the fewer interruptions. "And Lillian please go pack the tin Susan 'accidentally' left last time she was here."

Lillian blinked, then slid obediently after Sophie with a glance over her shoulder at the grown-ups. "We'll be right back. Don't let gossip while we're gone, it's my favorite part."

"Never," her grandmother winked at her. Lillian, only twelve years old but a true Greymoor girl at heart.

The door clicked. The room thinned by four, and the rest of the table obligingly shifted conversations toward bunting yardage and the pie-eating contest, while Irene looked towards Mavis, cocked her head, and whispered a few words.

Agnes set down her needles, finally looked at June. "Well?"

June's eyes were bright, but her voice was calm as rain. "He belongs. The place knows him."

"You're certain?" Irene asked.

Sybil leaned forward, bracelets singing very faintly. "Certain as bells on a sleigh. He was called."

Roland scowled at the corner again. "Door opened for him by itself. That's not nothing."

"It's true." Ruth confirmed.

Agnes's mouth relaxed, the way it did when the pattern she'd been counting resolved exactly where she hoped. "The shop opened the door."

Nell nodded. "And the book. The old one at the inn. It found him. He's reading what belongs to your line."

"Does he know?" Irene said.

"Of course not," Beatrix said, exasperated and fond. "Men who are worth anything rarely know the reason for their arrival."

Agnes sat back. Relief—sharp and unexpected—cut through her like a draw of clean air. Not because her niece needed a man to be complete; because she had watched her niece paddling alone for so long it was a mercy to learn the wave of change had arrived to carry her forward, not tip her over.

"And Max?" Irene asked, eyes soft thinking of her grandson.

June's expression did something so gentle it made the room feel briefly holy. "The boy will be deeply loved. The bond is already beginning in the small things."

"Good," Agnes said simply. "Then we will help the small things along."

The door opened. The girls returned with unnecessary peppermint and an old tin Susan had "accidentally" overfilled with biscotti a few weeks back. Agnes picked up her needles like nothing had happened.

"What'd we miss?" Lillian asked.

"Mae upset Dorothy by calling crochet 'knitting's chaotic cousin,'" Irene said smoothly.

"Accurate," Mae said.

"Heretical," Dorothy sniffed

Irene glanced at Mavis and gave a subtle wink in her direction.

Mavis, blissfully oblivious to any pronouncements about the condition of her heart—thanks to her mother—tried to cast on and somehow made a figure eight. "This yarn is an agent of chaos."

"It's the courage colorway," Agnes said.

Mavis glanced up. "Is that... a thing?"

"It is tonight," Agnes said, and that was that.

They fell back into the business of the evening. Lydia smoothed salve onto Dorothy's knuckle and muttered something about frankincense. The kettle refilled itself when Irene turned her back—and if she sent a pleased look to June, no one remarked on it. Nibs, bored with decorum, batted a scrap of acrylic under a shelf and then pretended he hadn't. Emma and Tansy counted stitches aloud, then whispered over whose lantern would look best with tassels. Sybil set three stitch markers in a perfect triangle around Mavis's cast-on and said, "So you won't lose your place while you're staring at a man."

"Sybil!" Beatrix said, scandalized only in performance.

"I am a realist," Sybil replied.

Chuckles came from around the table while Mavis rolled her eyes.

They planned the Autumn Festival in joyful, inefficient detail. Dorothy insisted the historical scavenger hunt include the brass plaque behind the town hall because "half of learning is looking up," and Mae advocated for a cider refill station "because children are cups with legs." Ruth and Nell tried to calculate how many gallons of cocoa an inn can make before the pot revolts, and Lydia volunteered a warming tincture "for the stubborn and underdressed." Agnes drew bunting diagrams with the severity of a general mapping a campaign. Irene sketched out the lantern walk route with notes like "Hank's ladder—avoid—still sulking."

"Speaking of Hank," Mae said, "is his cow real?"

"Which cow?" Dorothy asked.

"The statue," Mae said. "The one on the memorial stone behind the church."

"She was brave," June said, mouth tipping. "Lightning and all. She did not panic."

"Unlike Hank," Roland muttered.

The entire room laughed.

As the hour softened toward late, Ruth passed biscuits one last time. Nell, who had made peace with her scarf's rebellious nature, draped it around her shoulders and declared it "textured." Dorothy finished a sock and immediately cast on its mate like a woman who knew second-sock syndrome was a moral failure. Emma and Tansy, high on the pride of ten straight stitches that looked like a road, took a triumphant selfie with Agnes dead-center scowling in the background in a way that made the photo perfect.

Mavis's phone buzzed—a text from Max from Susan's phone: IVY SAYS WE NEED MORE GLUE STICKS FOR LANTERN PRACTICE!!!! PLS. Also do I have to shower tonight.

She texted back: Yes re: shower. Ask Susan about glue sticks.

A beat. Then: Susan says shower is tyranny but ok.

Mavis smiled, pocketed the phone, and looked around the room. It was impossible not to feel the shape of her life here— the people who knew where her spare house key lived and which books she read when she was sad. She cast on again. The first five stitches settled, neat and obedient. The sixth drifted, then found its own mark as if some invisible hand had nudged it into place.

"Show-off," Mavis whispered to the air, eyes warm.

Beatrix, down the table, did not look up, but the corner of her mouth answered.

Irene tapped her pencil against her list. "Final business. Volunteers for the pie-eating contest adjudication."

"Not me," Mae said. "I'll take the apple-weighing post. I refuse to be splattered for justice."

"I'll be a judge," Dorothy said. "I crave power."

"Of course you do," Ruth murmured.

Lydia volunteered Peter to help.

Agnes folded her pattern with military precision. "Meeting adjourned. Continue knitting until your shoulders tell you to stop. Clean up as though you were raised by Irene."

"Which some of you were," Irene said, smug and sipping.

Chairs scraped; wool rustled. June rose without making the air colder. Beatrix stacked two abandoned patterns into order with a gesture that would have been a snap if she had the type of fingers that did such things. Sybil tucked the brave-red skein into Mavis's tote without so much as a flourish; the color settled there like a promise. Roland, on his way out, nudged Nibs with the toe of his boot-that-wasn't, and the cat, affronted in principle, allowed it.

On the way to the door, Lydia paused beside Agnes. "Do you trust him?" she asked her mother softly.

Agnes let one hand briefly cover Lydia's where it rested on the table. "I'm going to try."

"Do I worry?"

"You never do," Agnes said. "Keep that up."

Lydia's smile was quick and knowing. "As you command."

Mavis pulled on her coat and glanced out the window. The square beyond glowed with lamplight; a few early leaves— bravest among them—skated past like small flags. Agnes and Irene watched her without staring. It was a family trick.

"Need a walk home?" Irene asked, the way she always did.

"I'm good," Mavis said, which they knew meant: I'm happy.

"Take the red," Agnes said, nodding at the tote.

Mavis looked inside, puzzled. "Did I buy that?"

"You will," Agnes said.

Mavis laughed and kissed her aunt's cheek. "Bossy."

"Efficient," Agnes corrected.

The bell gave a modest chime as Mavis stepped out, the night greeting her with that particular Maplewick hush—quiet, but never empty.

Inside, as the door settled, Agnes exhaled. Irene's hand found hers, brief and steady.

"She'll be alright," Irene said.

"She will," Agnes agreed, eyes on the place where the skein had come from. "The town has decided. And so," she added, softer, "have we."

Outside, Mavis walked down the lane toward the square, tote snug to her hip. In the lamplight, the yarn shimmered a tiny glint like a wink. For the smallest second, a thread-thin line of light unspooled from the skein, curved in the air in the shape of a heart, and vanished immediately after.

Mavis paused, smiling without knowing why, and kept going.

Behind her, The Knittery settled back into itself. The kettle sighed its last, the swift stilled, the cubbies held their breaths like choristers waiting for the next note. The ghosts, satisfied, slipped back to the churchyard.

And Maplewick—old, attentive, confident—counted stitches, counted blessings, and made quiet room for what was coming.

Chapter Twelve

Some people avoided town meetings like the plague. Julian, on the other hand, brought a fresh notebook.

He arrived five minutes early, already flustered from having nearly tripped over a black cat on his way in (who looked like it was guarding the door). The Maplewick Town Hall building was modest—white clapboard, creaky steps, and an old chimney that leaned slightly to the left from age—but inside, it buzzed with anticipation and the smell of too many cinnamon breath mints.

Chairs were already being arranged in neat rows. The stub of chalk scraped softly across the blackboard in front of Maplewick Town Hall, looping neat letters into place though no hand held it. Words unfurled in a looping script, line after line appearing as if written by invisible hands:

Autumn Festival Planning Meeting
8:00 PM | All Welcome
Hot Cider & Optimism Provided

The last curl of the *d* in *Provided* settled into place just as Julian Everett stepped onto the creaky front steps, oblivious.

The final word settled with a faint shimmer of dust before the chalk dropped back into its tray, as if it had finished its evening's duty.

Julian took a seat in the second row, next to a very serious-looking woman knitting something the color of squash soup. He pulled out his pen and notebook, then promptly dropped the pen. When he bent to grab it, his notebook slid off his lap and landed squarely beneath the knitting needles.

The woman handed it back to him without a word, only the mildest raise of one eyebrow, and a nod after her eyes took him in and realized who he was.

Across the room, he spotted Mavis entering with Ruth and Susan, who were still mid-conversation about how many gallons of spiced cider the bakery could actually produce without burning out the heating element.

Lydia was talking to her husband, Peter, near the refreshments table, while Nell and Owen were helping the mayor set up the microphone—clearly pros at this.

Julian waved awkwardly to Mavis, who gave him a small smile and a nod. His stomach did a little loop.

Cool. Smooth. Incredibly professional.

The room filled quickly with more townsfolk—an older gentleman in suspenders named Hank, who brought his own folding chair because he didn't trust chairs that looked like "government-issued seating," and a pair of teenage twins from the high school who sat at the back whispering furiously about who would be running the caramel apple booth.

Mayor Tilly Newell, a compact woman with wild gray curls and enviable posture, called the meeting to order by tapping a wooden spoon on a thermos.

"Alright, friends," she said brightly. "We're six weeks out from the Autumn Festival. Our first full town gathering since mid-summer, and we intend to impress. Apple bobbing. Craft tents. A hayride with slightly improved seating. Let's get planning."

Nods all around.

Principal Moreno stood and adjusted her glasses. "Briar Ridge students will be hosting the historical scavenger hunt again this year, along with the elementary art display. I'll be sending home sign-up sheets next week, and we'll need a few volunteers for booth support."

Mavis scribbled a note on the back of the flyer in her lap. Max had already been talking about desperately wanting her to help at a candy corn booth.

The mayor consulted her clipboard. "We still need volunteers for setup and cleanup, a few booth coordinators, and someone brave enough to organize the pie-eating contest, though we now have our judges. Thank you to Dorothy and Peter for volunteering to help me at the judging table! The budget has room for hay bales, but *not* for pumpkin trebuchets, no matter what Sam Ryder tries to claim on the expense report."

Someone in the back groaned.

Julian raised his hand and cleared his throat. "Excuse me, uh... what's a pumpkin trebuchet?"

Everyone turned.

Ruth stage-whispered, "It's a catapult, dear."

"Oh," he said. "Of course. That tracks."

He sank slightly lower in his chair, but Mavis gave him a look—half amused, half fond—that helped his pride limp upright again.

The meeting continued with cheerful debate over cider portions, booth locations, and whether or not the banjo trio should be allowed to play all six verses of "The Maplewick Harvest Song." Julian took notes. He probably didn't need to. But he liked the rhythm of it—the way this town cared about its traditions like they were living things. The way people had opinions about seating charts and cider spice ratios because it all mattered.

It reminded him of the other old towns he'd read about over the years. The ones that survived because their people wanted them to.

He snuck another glance at Mavis, who was now whispering something to her sister, Ruth, both of them trying not to laugh.

He had a feeling this one might be the town that mattered to him, too.

ই ই ই

After the meeting, the family slowly trickled toward the door in clumps. Agnes and Irene were holding cider cups and talking with Lydia and Peter about how to label hand-knit items at the craft table.

Julian approached Mavis as she folded her chair. "We're all headed to the Inn." She said, brushing a strand of hair behind her ear. "Nell's oldest was watching the kids for the evening, so I'm just heading back to grab Max. Want to walk with us?"

He adjusted his notebook under his arm. "Perfect. Maybe you can help me process what I've just learned about a small New England town that is capable of building medieval weaponry out of scrap wood and determination."

Mavis grinned. "Wait until you see what they do with the apple slingshots."

They stepped out into the cool evening air, the scent of chimney smoke and distant pine hanging on the breeze. The town square glowed softly under string lights still hung from summer—soon to be swapped for autumn bunting and lanterns. Julian tucked his hands into his coat pockets and let the quiet stretch between them as they walked.

He felt... steady.

Like this place had a rhythm, and he was starting to learn it.

And beside him, Mavis walked like she'd always been part of that rhythm. And maybe, if he stayed long enough, he could learn how to belong, too.

❧ ❧ ❧

The front steps of the Maplewick Inn glowed in the amber light of the lanterns, still warm with the chatter of town hall. Mavis paused with Julian at the base of the porch, waiting for the rest of the family to catch up. Behind them, Lydia and Peter strolled hand-in-hand, deep in quiet conversation. Ruth and Susan trailed just behind, Ruth gesturing animatedly about one of the booths and Susan laughing softly. Nell and Owen were mid-discussion about pumpkin storage logistics, which somehow sounded more serious than it probably was.

The group climbed the stairs together, a cozy swarm of scarves, chuckles, and familiarity.

Owen held the door for everyone. "I think that meeting set a new record for cider consumption and number of debates about extension cords."

"Don't forget the glitter controversy," Peter added. "Maplewick's annual scandal."

"Some of us are still cleaning up from last year," Lydia said, brushing a phantom fleck off her coat.

Inside, the inn was warm and glowing with lamplight. Jonah Hale, Nell and Owen's eldest, looked up from the sitting room, gave a wave, and said, "They're in the sunroom."

Mavis led the way down the hall, Julian keeping pace beside her.

They found Max at the puzzle table, Ivy beside him, holding a corner piece aloft with great reverence. Benji sat on the floor nearby, Sophie and Lillian helping him separate edge pieces, all of them eating apple slices from the same bowl.

"We're basically geniuses now," Max announced. "Four corners and two whole sides."

"Gifted children, clearly," Mavis said, ruffling his hair.

Susan crouched to give Ivy and Benji quick kisses on their heads. "Time to head back, loves. Say goodnight."

There were hugs and high-fives all around. Mavis held open Max's coat for him and gathered his sketchpad while the cousins corralled their kids, coats, and leftover puzzle pieces.

"We'll see you tomorrow for the planning meeting," Nell said, walking everyone to the door. "Breakfast at Ruth's?"

"Obviously," Ruth said. "Cinnamon scones. Susan's baking."

"Pumpkin cinnamon," Susan added, clearly pleased.

The front hallway buzzed with soft goodbyes, zippers, and the rustle of scarves as one family after another stepped into the evening.

Julian lingered just behind Mavis as she adjusted Max's backpack over her shoulder.

He cleared his throat. "Would you mind if I walked you home?"

Mavis looked up at him, surprised.

Julian smiled, a little sheepishly. "I'm not ready to settle in for the night yet. Plus, I enjoy your company."

Max, already halfway out the door, piped up, "He can carry my backpack if I get tired."

Julian laughed. "That seems fair."

Mavis smiled. "We'd like that."

They stepped out into the cool evening air, the scent of chimney smoke and distant pine hanging on the breeze. The town square glowed softly under string lights still hung from summer—soon to be swapped for autumn leaves and lanterns.

Just beneath one of the old lampposts the black cat with bright copper eyes sat neatly on the cobblestones, tail curled around its paws like it was standing guard. It blinked once, slow and deliberate, before slipping into the shadows between buildings.

Julian frowned. "That's... twice now."

"That's Nibs," Mavis said lightly.

Julian gave her a sidelong glance, half amused, half unsettled, but said nothing more.

The walk was quiet at first. Max skipped a few paces ahead, narrating aloud the progress of his puzzle like a sports commentator.

Julian tucked his hands into his coat pockets and glanced over at Mavis. "So, are they always like that?" He nodded towards the Town Hall.

"What, town meetings?" Mavis asked.

Julian nodded. "More baked goods than bureaucracy?"

"Maplewick runs on snacks and strong opinions," she said. "The cider helps take the edge off."

"I was warned small towns were political," he said. "I just didn't realize the glitter lobby was so aggressive."

"Oh, you haven't even seen the wreath wars yet," Mavis said. "That starts in November. People mysteriously 'misplace' each other's door decorations. It's festive... and mildly criminal."

Julian laughed. "And here I was worried about remembering names. I should be worried about sabotage."

"You should be worried about Nell. She can organize a potluck and a public uprising in the same afternoon, and Christmas is her favorite holiday." She paused and then softly added, "not that you'll be here for her shenanigans, I guess."

"We'll see." Julian gave her a half smile. "Noted. Never cross the woman with the color-coded clipboard."

"Wise man."

They reached the bookshop, and Max bounded up ahead.

"I'm getting my pajamas," he announced. "Then a snack!"

Mavis turned to Julian. "Thanks for walking with us."

He hesitated just a moment, then smiled. "I'll see you tomorrow?"

She nodded, her heart warm. "Yeah. You will."

As she and Max slipped into the shop, Julian stood for a moment longer under the lamplight, something about the quiet street and the cozy glow behind the bookshop windows making him feel anchored.

Maybe even home.

Chapter Thirteen

The best meetings ended with leftover cookies and a child trying to negotiate a sleepover.

All four women were tucked around Ruth and Susan's kitchen table, teacups half-full, clipboards askew, and a mostly-demolished plate of cardamom snickerdoodles in the center. A beeswax candle flickered beside a small vase of late-summer sunflowers, and someone—probably Nell—had refilled everyone's mugs without asking.

They were wrapping up another round of retreat planning, voices low and familiar, the way they always got after a couple of hours together. Lydia had begun untangling a skein of yarn she'd pulled from her bag, Ruth was sketching out the bakery's prep timeline on the back of the to-do list, Nell was still trying to finish her final notes even though the conversation had long since wandered, and Mavis leaned back in her chair, eyes soft, feeling something like peace settle into her chest.

Susan passed through with a tray of fresh apple cinnamon oatmeal cookies she'd "just happened" to make.

"Accidentally baked," she said, setting them down. "Tragic."

"You're doing the Lord's work," Lydia murmured, already reaching for one.

They laughed. There was always something about these meetings that made everything feel manageable again—like no matter what happened, they had each other, and tea, and a to-do list that somehow always got done.

From the living room came a thud and a suspicious silence.

"Max?" Mavis called.

"I'm okay!" his voice called back. "That was Ivy's fault!"

"No it wasn't!" Ivy's voice followed, indignant.

Ruth didn't even flinch. "At least no one's crying," she said serenely.

A few minutes later, the meeting dissolved, and Lydia and Nell stood to leave. Mavis gathered her notes, already knowing what was coming.

"Please?" Max asked, darting into the kitchen like he'd been waiting for the moment the grown-ups broke rank. "Just an hour. Ivy said I could help her build a fort, and Benji's got the good crayons."

"I do," Benji said proudly, holding up a tin like it was buried treasure.

Mavis raised an eyebrow. "Are they crayons or the souls of kings?"

"Crayons," Benji said after a thoughtful pause. "But really good ones."

Susan chuckled from the sink. "They'll be fine here. I have snacks, a stopwatch, and a healthy fear of Ruth's disapproving face if I let them run wild."

"Hey," Ruth said, though she didn't actually look offended. "My face is very reasonable."

"You're sure?" Mavis asked, glancing between Susan and Ruth.

"Go," Ruth said. "Take a moment of peace. That's an order."

Mavis bent to kiss the top of Max's head. "One hour. If I come back and you've dyed your hair with blueberry jam again—"

"That was one time," Max groaned.

"It was your cousin's idea," Ivy added, shrugging, looking over at Lydia who smirked before calling goodbye over her shoulder.

Mavis gave them all a look and gathered her things, the last one to leave. She stepped outside and let the cottage door close gently behind her, the sudden hush of early evening settling like a shawl around her shoulders.

As she started down the path, two familiar figures came into view—her mother and Aunt Agnes, walking arm in arm toward Ruth's front gate, their heads bent close in quiet conversation.

"Evening, love," Irene called warmly, lifting her free hand in greeting.

Mavis smiled, pausing just long enough to hug her mother and aunt before continuing down the lane.

Once she had passed, the sisters slowed. Agnes lifted her hand toward the sky, then wiggled her fingers, like brushing flour from them. Irene gave a knowing little wink.

The clouds above shifted, darkening at the edges. A cool breath of air rolled down the lane, and the first drop of rain landed on the back of Mavis's hand.

She glanced up, tugging her cardigan closer. Storm coming, she thought.

Behind her, Irene and Agnes exchanged smiles, Irene glancing over her shoulder at her daughter, and carried on toward the cottage.

The leaves above the path rustled in a cooler breeze, and the scent of rain rode in beneath it—fresh, earthy, and familiar. Mavis pulled her cardigan tighter and set off down the quiet lane toward home. As she walked, the first scattered drops of rain began to fall—light and occasional, like the sky hadn't quite made up its mind yet. She tilted her head back and watched the dark clouds gathering over Maplewick's steeples and rooftops.

It looked like something was coming.

The rain was beginning to fall in earnest by the time Mavis rounded the corner to the square. Maplewick was quiet in that particular way small towns became during a storm—shop signs creaked gently in the wind, windows glowed softly behind drawn curtains, and the wet cobblestones glistened like spilled ink.

She climbed the stairs to the bookshop, fishing her key from her cardigan pocket. But when she stepped inside, the bell above the door gave a curious little jingle—followed by a familiar voice.

"I was wondering when you'd get back."

Julian stood from one of the velvet armchairs near the poetry section, setting aside a thick book that Mavis instantly recognized as the Maplewick history volume he'd mentioned on their walk. He looked sheepish, rain-damp at the shoulders, curls slightly tousled, and absolutely at home.

"I hope this isn't strange," he said, pushing his glasses up the bridge of his nose. "Well—it is strange. But I was walking past and saw the lights were off, assumed you were out, but then... the door sort of... opened itself."

Mavis blinked. "It did?"

He gave a half-laugh. "Yeah. Just unlatched and swung open. I stood there awkwardly for a minute, trying to decide if it was an elaborate trap—or a very confident invitation—and then it just... shut behind me."

She raised an eyebrow, stepping fully into the shop and closing her umbrella. "And you came in anyway?"

He shrugged. "I've learned not to question too much in Maplewick."

"Good instinct," she said, amused.

"I figured the worst that could happen was a haunted copy of Wuthering Heights pelting me from the shelves. And anyway, once I was inside, I admit, it was nice to have an escape from the starting rain.."

The lights were soft, one of the reading lamps glowing near the armchair. The air smelled like lemon balm and worn paper—Hattie's signature touch when she'd tidied earlier. Mavis set her bag down behind the counter and crossed to where Julian was standing.

He gestured to the book. "I brought this. It's the one I told you about that was left on the little table in my room, and I couldn't put it down. There's no title page, no author name—just this ridiculously detailed account of Maplewick's history. It reads like a mix of academic research and firsthand storytelling, but some of the details go right up to this decade. Which makes no sense."

Mavis leaned over to glance at the pages, heart thudding a little faster—not from nerves, but from recognition. She knew this book. Knew its quiet pulse, the way it continued growing through the generations. Every Whitlock town historian added to it, in careful script. And now it was hers. But it had disappeared a few weeks ago, as it does, and now she knew why.

"I'd love to take a look," she said, voice gentle, playing along.

Julian studied her for a moment, then nodded, passing it into her hands.

Before she could speak again, thunder rumbled overhead—low and long. The lights flickered, then steadied. Rain pelted the windows in earnest now, quickening against the panes and echoing softly through the shop.

Mavis glanced toward the door. "You might be stuck here for a bit."

Julian looked amused rather than concerned. "Worse places to be trapped. Does it often storm like this here?"

"Sometimes," she said, settling onto the arm of a nearby chair, the book still in her hands. "When it does... it usually means something."

Julian tilted his head. "Something magical?"

Mavis gave a noncommittal smile. "Something memorable."

Thunder rolled again, and somewhere upstairs, the pipes groaned faintly. The bookshop felt even smaller and more sacred than usual; wrapped in stormlight and stories.

Julian looked at her, eyes curious but kind. "You sure you don't mind me being here?"

"I'm sure," she said, meaning it.

He relaxed into the opposite chair, draping his arm along the back as if he'd been coming to this shop for years.

And with the rain thickening and the lights warm, the book between them, Mavis had the sudden, quiet wish that he had been.

The storm wasn't passing. If anything, it was swelling; dark clouds pressing low against the windows, thunder rumbling louder, the rain falling harder. It felt like the whole town had paused.

శు శు శు

Julian had moved to the armchair beside Mavis's desk, long legs stretched out and a mug of tea in his hands. A lamp glowed between them, casting golden light against the shadows, as if the bookshop itself were holding its breath.

He glanced at her, his voice low. "Can I ask about Max's dad?"

Mavis didn't hesitate. "Sure."

Julian waited.

She traced her finger around the rim of her mug. "It wasn't a relationship, really. It was a moment. One of those whirlwind things that leaves you dizzy, not steady. He was passing through

Maplewick. He was charming, magnetic, and gone before I could even take a breath."

Julian's brow furrowed gently. "Did he know?"

"He knew. He just didn't ask what came next. And by the time I could wrap my head around the fact that I was pregnant, he was already gone. No forwarding address, no goodbye. Just... vanished." She shrugged. "Max and I have never needed him. We've always had each other. And this town... they've held us like we belonged here all along."

Julian's face softened with something that looked like admiration. "You didn't let it harden you."

"I was cracked for a while," she admitted. "But not ruined."

Silence stretched, the comforting kind. The rain deepened, beating harder on the windows. A gust rattled the front door.

"Your turn," Mavis said, tilting her head toward him. "Any big, dramatic love stories of your own?"

Julian chuckled, slow and quiet. "A few undramatic ones. I've dated—here and there. But mostly, I've been in a long-term relationship with academia. Grad school, research grants, guest lectures. I've moved so often I kept my spices in a Ziploc bag for years."

Mavis laughed, the kind that made her shoulders drop. "Romantic."

"I know." He grinned. "It's hard to build something real when you're always packing it up again. I kept telling myself I was too busy for love. Too focused, and my career came easier to me than navigating relationships did."

She looked at him then, not with sympathy, but something warmer. Something more curious.

"And now?"

Julian met her gaze. "Now I think I'm done being afraid."

The rain pulsed like a second heartbeat. The air between them thickened; not just with storm humidity, but with something slower, heavier, unspoken.

Mavis stood to gather their mugs, but Julian reached for her hand—his fingers warm, steady.

The moment stretched.

She didn't pull away.

He didn't speak.

He was close enough now that she could smell him—earthy and clean, like cedar and old books and something herbal. A quiet kind of masculine. The kind that crept up gentle but strong.

When she looked up, he was already watching her.

Not just watching, wanting. Not impatient or demanding. Just present. Clear. As if he'd already decided he would wait as long as she needed.

Her breath caught.

She leaned in before she could talk herself out of it.

And when he kissed her—softly, reverently, like he wasn't just kissing her but learning her—Mavis felt something open.

His hand came to rest gently at the small of her back, anchoring her there as the storm swelled outside. And she kissed him back, her heart fluttering and steady all at once.

When they parted, neither said anything for a moment.

There was only the storm. And the steady warmth between them.

Mavis breathed in slowly, and felt something she hadn't in years—safe and seen, all at once.

And wanted.

Julian's hand lingered at her back, warm and steady, his eyes still on her like he was memorizing the moment. Mavis pulled in a breath, but it caught halfway.

She hadn't realized how much she wanted—craved—being wanted. Not just as a mother or business owner or dependable friend. But as a woman.

She felt it now, clear as day. The way Julian looked at her made her feel lightheaded.

He was so much more handsome than she'd let herself admit. His hair was a little unruly and soft-looking, the kind of hair she imagined running her fingers through without permission. His jaw had that slightly scruffy shadow that made her stomach flutter more than she wanted to admit. And his eyes—gray with flecks of green—looked at her in a way that was almost unbearable.

She wanted more.

More time, more talking, more... kissing.

Julian stepped back a fraction, and Mavis almost pulled him back, she wanted the solid warmth of his body. "I haven't felt pulled to someone like this in a long time," he said quietly.

She looked up at him, heart thudding. "Same."

The storm outside was beginning to shift. The thunder grew distant, the rain softening to a whisper on the windows. Light began to peek through the clouds; dim, golden-edged. The kind that made the world feel washed clean.

They stood in the hush, not quite ready to return to real life.

But the bell above the shop door chimed soft and familiar.

A moment later, children's voices filled the stairwell.

"We're back!" Ivy called. "And it stopped raining!"

"Barely!" Benji yelled. "My shoes are still squishy!"

Mavis blinked, the spell broken in the gentlest way.

Susan's voice followed from behind them. "We're reopening the bakery in ten!"

Julian smiled, brushing a hand through his hair. "Duty calls."

Mavis gave a rueful little laugh. "It always does."

They shared one more look, soft and full of something new. Then Mavis turned toward the front counter, cheeks flushed and heart unsteady in the best way.

Chapter Fourteen

The morning after the storm was washed in that particular kind of golden light that made Maplewick look as if it had been hand-painted; every leaf a little sharper, every shadow a little softer. The air carried the faintest scent of damp pine and woodsmoke, lingering from the night before.

Max tugged on his backpack, already halfway out the apartment door.

"Susan's waiting!" he called. "We're walking today."

"Have fun," Mavis said, smoothing his collar as he darted past her. "And remember—"

"I know," he groaned good-naturedly. "Look both ways, don't run ahead, be nice to my cousins."

"Exactly." She bent to kiss the top of his head. "See you this afternoon."

He gave her a lopsided grin before bounding down the stairs to where Susan, Ivy, and Benji were waiting. Mavis watched from the upstairs window as the little group headed down the street, Max already talking animatedly with his hands while Benji tried to keep up. She loved him so much it almost hurt.

The bookshop was quiet as she came down the stairs and turned on the lamps that Hattie had left off. Mavis had just settled at the front counter when the connecting door to the bakery swung open and Ruth leaned against the frame, holding two steaming mugs of tea like peace offerings.

"Storm survivors get first pick," Ruth announced.

Mavis grinned. "You're very magnanimous for someone who probably just stole the last of the blueberry scones."

Ruth stepped inside and set one mug in front of her. "You can't prove that."

"I can if I check the display case."

"You could... or you could drink your tea and enjoy this beautiful morning without accusing your sister of pastry crimes."

Mavis rolled her eyes but took a sip. "What's in it for me?"

"Well..." Ruth's eyes narrowed just enough to make Mavis suspicious. "How about that "alone" time last night during the storm? You seem a little brighter today."

"Brighter?"

"Yeah. Storm's gone, and you've got that glow—like you've been out walking in fresh air... or, you know, locking up the shop with a certain historian inside."

Mavis gave her a flat look. "You're impossible."

"It's my job as a younger sister," Ruth corrected, leaning on the counter across from Mavis. "And I know that face. That's the 'someone made me tea without asking' face... only, judging by your grin, they kissed you first."

Mavis snorted into her tea. "You are ridiculous."

"And you're not denying it."

Mavis tried, and failed, to smother a smile. "Drink your tea and go mind your bakery."

Ruth slid back from the counter with a little shrug, still smirking. "Fine, fine. But just remember—little sisters get first dibs on details."

"Not happening," Mavis called after her.

"Mm-hmm," Ruth's voice floated back through the closing door. "We'll see."

Mavis shook her head, the corners of her mouth still curved in spite of herself. She turned to glance out the window again, noticing the way the light was already shifting. Out toward the square, a bank of dark clouds had begun to gather low on the horizon, moving faster than she liked. It looked as though the day might change its mind.

She turned the sign to OPEN and exhaled.

❧ ❧ ❧

Julian arrived just after ten with his notebook and a cautious, hopeful grin. He paused inside the door like a person arriving in a dream he'd had before.

"Morning," he said.

"Hi." Her smile curved before she could help it.

He lifted a canvas bag. "I brought something weird."

"That's my favorite category."

He laid a clothbound book on the counter—nineteenth-century bindings, copperplate initials on the flyleaf, a tiny watercolor of the square tucked between pages. "Found it in a box of donated odds and ends at the inn. Ledger from the old general store with someone's marginalia. Recipes, receipts, and five separate notes about Sam Ryder's historical 'improvements' to the hay wagon."

Mavis laughed. "There were casualties."

"I thought you might want it for the shop. Or to use with your... tour guiding."

He said it lightly, but his eyes were careful, like he wasn't sure where the edges of last night landed in daylight.

"Thank you," she said, equally careful. "I do."

For a second they stood there smiling at each other, caught between what they were and whatever they were becoming.

Julian cleared his throat. "I'm walking the ridge trail tomorrow to look at the old mill site. Do you—would you like to come?"

"Yes," she said, quicker than she meant to. "I'd like that."

His shoulders eased, a smile spreading across his face. "Good, me too."

He lingered, flipping the ledger open, admiration clear in his voice as they paged through the looping script together. She loved the way he looked at things—how his mind arrived with a pencil and a cup of patience. After a minute, he closed the book and glanced toward the window.

"I should let you work," he said. "My own pile is waiting."

"Come back later," she said, and it wasn't a question.

"I will."

When the bell chimed again, he was gone, and the shop felt empty in a new way.

రు రు రు

The rest of the morning slid into place: a retired couple looking for gardening memoirs; a college student asking where the poetry started ("There," Mavis said, "and there, and it creeps over here when it's feeling bold"). Between customers, she began on the retreat book bundles, pulling stacks for the guests.

"Grief," she murmured, setting aside a slim volume with a tender spine that had floated over. "Change." A novel with a kitchen at its heart slid off of the shelf. "Permission." An essay collection made its way to her.

A paperback slid from a higher shelf and landed neatly by her elbow.

Mavis glanced up, amused. "Show-off."

Another book eased forward and thunked into the first— *Poems for People In Love.* It fell open to a handful of lines about being seen and choosing to stay. Mavis's throat went warm. She read the lines twice, then tucked the slim volume carefully into her pocket to read more thoroughly later.

"Thank you," she said to a room that while looking empty to most people housed a very special Hattie who cared so much about Mavis.

The bell chimed now and then; she rang up a cookbook, three mysteries, a stack of used paperbacks that smelled like someone's attic. Time fogged a little in that cozy, bookish way until the afternoon brightened behind the windows and it was nearly time for school to let out.

Max barreled in at three with Ivy and Benji, crumb-dusted and happy. "We're signing up for booth shifts!" he reported. "I picked 'Guess the Candy Corn' and Ivy says we should do lantern crafts and Benji says—"

"Pumpkin catapult!" Benji crowed.

"No trebuchets," Mavis said gently, falling into laughter with them anyway. They sprawled at the homework table, then ping-ponged back into the bakery with Ivy's earnest plans to steal one celebratory cookie for "brain fuel" for each other them.

The shop settled again when they'd gone, the late sun slanting across the floorboards, the air smelling faintly of lemon and cinnamon. Mavis finished a note to tuck into one of the bundles—two sentences that said more than they had any right to—and set it aside with a little weight in her heart.

135

At closing, she flicked the sign to closed and stepped outside with a cup of tea. The sky was shedding its blue, turning itself toward gold. Lights blinked on across the square. SHe could hear the kids at the table with Beatrix while leaned against the doorframe, the wood warm at her back, and let her thoughts go where they wanted.

Julian. The way his smile arrived like sunlight. The careful questions. The kiss—steady, sweet, like an answer to a question she hadn't known she'd asked. She turned the cup in her hands and admitted, at least to herself, how much she was beginning to like him. Not a rush, not a tumble—something surer. Something she wanted to spend time inside of.

The church bell across the way chimed the hour; soft and familiar. Mavis finished her tea and headed up to the apartment to start dinner, the laughter from the homework table drifting up the stairs behind her.

Chapter Fifteen

The next morning dawned bright, the air with that crispness that hinted at autumn even if the calendar insisted it was the last days of August. Mavis met Julian outside the inn just after nine. He was dressed for walking in well-worn boots, dark jeans and a flannel layered over a T-shirt. And he carried the same canvas bag he'd brought to the shop yesterday.

Nell appeared in the doorway behind him, holding out a cloth-wrapped bundle and a thermos.

"Provisions," she said. "If you're going to the ridge trail, you'll need more than a historian's enthusiasm to keep you upright."

Mavis laughed and took the bundle. "You didn't have to—"

"I wanted to," Nell said, her voice warm. "Go enjoy yourselves. And watch your step up by the mill site; the rocks are still slick from the storm."

They set off down the lane that led past the churchyard and toward the trailhead. The ground was soft underfoot, the scent of pine stronger after last night's rain.

As they walked, Mavis told him about the kids' growing plans for the Autumn Festival.

"Max wants to run the 'Guess the Candy Corn' booth," she said, smiling. "Ivy is all about lantern crafts, and Benji, well, Benji wants to build a pumpkin catapult."

Julian laughed. "That sounds about right."

"Thankfully, the committee has a 'no flying produce' rule, so we'll stick to pumpkins that stay in one place." She glanced sideways at him. "Do you think you'll still be here for it?"

"I hope so," he said without hesitation. "Maplewick has a way of making you want to stay."

The trail began to climb, roots threading across the earth. Sunlight flickered through the branches overhead. At one steeper section, Mavis's boot caught on a slick patch of moss, and she stumbled. Julian caught her elbow in a steady, sure grip.

"Got you," he said, his voice low but certain.

A faint shimmer curled between their joined hands—like a silver thread catching the morning light. Julian blinked at the brightness through the trees, dismissing it as sun on dew. But

Mavis felt the tug of her own magic, quick and sharp, before she quickly steadied herself.

She straightened, feeling the warmth of his hand even after he released it. "Thanks." She had been looking up, their eyes locked as she straightened herself. She wanted him to kiss her so much she almost felt like she conjured it when he leaned forward. She met him halfway, and his warm hand was on the small of her back again. She couldn't remember the last time kissing someone felt so natural and so comforting. Their conversations flowed so easily and now this too. Kissing Julian reminded her of his size and how he enveloped her into him as he held her, and his smell, lightly woody. She had forgotten how intoxicating a man's smell could be. She stepped back to take a breath and almost slipped again. Julian caught her and smiled, "I hope that was ok?"

"More than ok," she sighed.

They fell into an easy rhythm again, Julian stopping now and then to note a detail—a lichen-covered stone, the curve of an old fence post leaning into the undergrowth. Mavis told him the stories she knew: how the fence marked the edge of the old sheep pasture, how the storm of '62 had brought down half the pines along this ridge.

By the time they reached the overlook, the square below was a scatter of rooftops and the first hints of turning leaves. Mavis unwrapped Nell's bundle—thick slices of bread, a small jar of apple butter, two wedges of cheddar, and oatmeal cookies dotted with dried cranberries. The thermos held black tea that was still warm.

They sat on a flat rock with their knees touching. Mavis spread apple butter across her slice of bread and handed the jar to Julian. He accepted it with a wry smile. "Trail rations like these could convince me to take up hiking full time."

"Don't tell Nell that," she said. "She'll have you leading a breakfast hiking series before the week's out."

When they reached the old mill site, Julian walked the perimeter slowly, crouching to study the foundation stones and the moss that clung to them. The water ran steady through what had once been the sluice path, the sound mingling with the rush of wind through the trees.

Mavis rested her hands on the low wall. "They say one of the mill workers still hums here. He used to mend fishing nets between loads. Sometimes, if you come at dusk, you can hear it."

Julian glanced at her with a raised brow. "And have you heard it?"

"Once or twice," she admitted. "Could have been the water. Could have been something else."

As if on cue, a low, wavering note carried through the air. Just one, then gone—folded into the sound of the stream. Julian frowned slightly, cocking his head. "Strange echo."

Mavis only smiled.

He smiled back and there was a spark in his eyes as though he was tucking the memory away for later.

The walk back to town was quieter, not out of discomfort but because it seemed unnecessary to fill every space between them. Their shoulders brushed now and then, the kind of accidental contact neither of them stepped away from.

When they reached the square, Julian slowed outside the bakery. "Coffee?"

She smiled. "Yes and let's see if we can get one of Ruth's maple twist rolls before they're gone."

Inside, Ruth glanced between them, her mouth quirking just slightly. She slid two rolls into a plate and passed them across the counter without comment.

Steam curled from the pastries in the cool air—and for the briefest moment, it shaped itself into a heart before fading. Mavis's eyes flicked to Ruth, a knowing spark in her expression, but she said nothing.

They took their coffee and rolls to a corner table, the windows spilling late-morning light across the wood. Mavis broke her roll in half and passed a piece to Julian.

"This was a good day," he said.

"It was." She let her gaze meet his for a moment longer than necessary. "And we didn't even get lost."

"That's because I had an excellent guide."

They lingered over their coffee, conversation weaving between history and small-town life, and something less easily named kept finding its way into the spaces between their words; keeping the conversation comfortably flowing.

As they stood to leave, Julian reached for her coat from the back of her chair. His hand brushed hers as he passed it to her— just a brief, warm touch, but enough to send a spark up her spine.

Mavis smiled, pulling the coat around her.

For a moment neither of them moved, the hum of the bakery fading into the background. Then he tipped his head toward the door, and they stepped out into the cool air together. The sky was clear, but the wind held the edge of the season to come.

The walk toward the Inn was unhurried, their shoulders brushing now and then. Mavis found she liked the pace— unrushed and steady—like the kind of conversation that didn't need to prove itself.

Outside the Inn, Julian slowed. "I'll head up and get some work done," he said. "Try not to eat my share of those rolls before tomorrow."

She smiled. "No promises."

Inside, the parlor was warm and smelled faintly of cinnamon. Max was at a table with Ivy and Benji, bent over a game of checkers while his aunt Susan read in the armchair nearby. His face lit when he saw Mavis, and she felt the familiar, grounding tug of home.

Julian gave her a small nod before heading toward the staircase, and Mavis watched him go for an extra beat, wondering what it would be like to be heading upstairs with him, before turning to gather Max's things. Together, they stepped back out into the bright, brisk afternoon, the Inn's door swinging shut behind them.

Chapter Sixteen

Whitlock Books and Maple & Sage had become a single, sprawling workshop: long folding tables bridged open the dutch doors between bakery and bookshop, covered in brown craft paper and the kind of supplies that multiply when no one is looking—paper lantern kits, tissue leaves, jars of buttons, coils of twine, ribbon in audacious shades, a suspicious quantity of glitter, and three glue guns that Ruth kept eyeing like misbehaving appliances. A hand-lettered sign on the bakery's side read: FESTIVAL CRAFT DAY: COME GLUE A THING. Someone (almost certainly Agnes) had added a flourish of knitted vines to the corners.

Mavis stood by the window table assembling lantern prototypes, sleeves pushed to her elbows, a safety pin between her teeth. Max and Ivy flanked her, working on booth decorations: GUESS THE CANDY CORN in bold block letters. Benji, across from them, drew a pumpkin wearing a seatbelt.

"Safety," he said when no one asked.

"Correct," Susan replied, sliding him a plate of apple slices.

Ruth drifted past with a tray of cinnamon knots, offering them like bribes to the glue-gun gods. "If any of you so much as think about hot-gluing directly to the table, I will haunt you."

"Too late," said Mavis, deadpan. "We're already haunted."

"By poor choices?" Ruth asked.

"Also correct," Mavis said, and earned a snort from Susan.

Lydia arrived with a basket looped over one arm filled with spools of raffia, tiny clothespins, stamped tags, bottled patience. "Owen and Peter are hauling hay bales to the green," she announced, setting the basket down. "Which means we have exactly ninety minutes before they return and begin discussing 'structural integrity' of the craft tent."

"May heaven spare us from the phrase 'load-bearing garland,'" Ruth muttered.

The bell over the front door chimed, and Julian stepped in with that slightly wind-tossed look that made him appear like a man who'd been thinking while walking. He paused, taking in the tables, the organized wreckage, the small humans already speckled in gold.

"Welcome," Mavis said, smile rising without permission. "Choose a station: lanterns, signage, or glitter triage."

"Historian's choice?" Julian asked.

146

"Historian's penmanship," Mavis countered, tapping the blank poster board that waited for booth signs. "We need titles that look respectable enough to convince Principal Moreno we deserve an electrical outlet."

Julian set his notebook aside and rolled his sleeves. "I can letter respectably. Possibly even with moral authority."

"Perfect," Mavis said, handing him a pencil. "Start with CIDER & SPICE and PAPER LANTERN WORKSHOP. Benji, don't glue your sleeve."

Benji froze, eyes wide. "I would never glue my sleeve." He looked at Ruth. "Do we have sleeve covers, mom?"

Ruth tossed him one of Susan's spare baking cuffs. "Apron's cousin. Use it wisely."

A breeze slid across the floor from the poetry alcove and curled around Mavis's ankles—cool, soft, familiar. She didn't turn. "Afternoon, Hattie," she murmured, under her breath.

No one answered aloud, but the little hairs along Julian's forearm lifted as if he'd stepped into a patch of shade. He glanced toward the window. Closed. He shook it off and bent over the poster board, pencil moving with careful strokes.

"Max," Mavis said, "block letters, then outline. Ivy, caps consistent."

Ivy saluted with her marker. "Yes, ma'am."

Another small draft drifted through, lifting the corner of a stack of leaf-cutouts and turning one exactly the right way up. Mavis caught it with a fingertip, smiled, and set a small smooth stone on the pile.

"Who keeps moving the leaves?" Julian asked, more amused than concerned.

"Old building," Mavis said lightly. "Friendly cross-breeze."

"Extremely targeted cross-breeze," he murmured, but he was smiling.

Agnes and Irene appeared like a well-timed grandmotherly weather pattern, arms full of yarn, baskets of knitted bunting, and a tin labeled EMERGENCY BUTTONS in Irene's unwavering script.

"Ladies," Ruth said, "your timing is suspiciously perfect."

"It always has been," Irene replied, already sorting the bunting by color family. "Who's in charge of lantern strings?"

"Hattie," Mavis said automatically, then seeing Julian out of the corner of her eye and realizing her mistake, "Me. I am. Here." She lifted a spool of jute.

Julian's head tilted, the way it did when cataloguing. "Hattie?"

Mavis passed him a length of twine and sputtered, "family friend."

"That seems the general category for half the population," he said, not unkindly.

"It's a populous category," she agreed.

Max slid his sign closer to Julian. "Can you do the outline thing on this A?"

"Absolutely," Julian said, and did a crisp, tidy, and pleasing thickness that made the letter pop.

"Respectable," Max said with gravitas. "Almost principal-proof."

Julian bowed his head slightly. "High praise."

From the bakery side, Nell wandered in with a clipboard and a preternatural calm that could soothe stampeding toddlers and temperamental ovens. "Lantern kits accounted for," she announced. "Cider simmering. Glitter policy is still 'use with caution and remorse.'"

"We're not taking a stance on remorse," Lydia said. "That's between a person and their maker."

Benji raised a hand. "What's remorse?"

"Regret with extra feelings," Ruth said.

"Oh," Benji said, thoughtful. He glued a tasteful amount of glitter to the pumpkin's seatbelt.

A candle on the counter flickered once, as though a draft had found it. Mavis glanced up, eyes softening. Beatrix would be here soon; craft days were irresistible to a woman who valued correct margins.

"Max," Mavis said, "take a cookie run? Ask Susan for nine. Negotiate for six."

"Like a dragon," Max said, and jogged bakery-ward.

"Like a gentleman dragon," Mavis called after him. "Use your pleases."

Julian straightened, flexing his hand. "I will say," he murmured to Mavis, "there are worse ways to be indoctrinated into a town than letterheads and bunting."

"Crafting is Maplewick citizenship," Mavis said. "You glue a garland, you get a vote."

"Is that in the charter?"

"Unofficial bylaws," she said. "Irene keeps them."

"Of course she does."

Another faint breeze passed along the table edge, and a spool of ribbon spun an inch before stopping, its tail falling neatly toward Agnes's waiting fingers. She caught it without looking, as if someone had called her name.

"Thank you," Agnes said to the air with dry affection, then to Mavis, "Sybil says to not be stingy with the lanterns, they're her favorite part."

Mavis's mouth tilted. "Tell Sybil she owes me for the glitter."

"She says you owe her for her patience," Agnes replied, eyes twinkling.

Julian, on his third sign, looked up at the exchange and decided, reasonably, that the women in this family had a layered sense of humor that he liked very much but didn't always understand.

Benji held up the pumpkin. "Does a seatbelt need a buckle?"

"Always," Irene said. "Safety begins with a buckle."

"Safety," Benji echoed, reverent, and drew one carefully.

Max returned with cookies, like a conquering hero of baked goods. "Aunt Susan says we may have all nine on condition of sweeping when we're done!"

"That's called governance," Lydia said.

"Governance is delicious," Ivy said, selecting a cookie.

Julian slid one toward Mavis. Their fingers brushed. The smallest pause. He looked at her, and the bakery-and-bookshop clamor went soft around the edges for a second, like someone had turned down a single dial in a mix. She looked back— happy and steady, and a little amused because they had found a moment like this in the middle of a glue-stick uprising.

Max, noble destroyer of mood, said, "Mom, can we test the lanterns in the back room where it's darker?"

"Yes," Mavis said, smoothing a hand down his back. "One at a time. And no running with lit candles."

Julian glanced at her. "Is that in the charter?"

"Front page," she said.

The back room received a small convoy: Max, Ivy, two lanterns, and Lydia with a box of battery tea-lights because Lydia did not trust open flame with children who still thought glue was a condiment. When they switched them on, a warm hush fell and little circles of gold fell against the dim. Max made a pleased noise in his throat he would deny later.

"Bring them out," Mavis called. "We need to plan the canopy."

They did. Agnes began tying the first lantern onto a test line, fingers moving with the speed of someone who had strung a thousand party lights and survived to instruct others. A prickle of cool air lifted along the line as she reached. She tied the knot neatly. "You're right, Bea," she murmured to no one Julian could see. "Parallel, not staggered."

Julian looked up at the ceiling and then back at Mavis with a *did you hear that?* expression he tried to disguise as a smile. Mavis shrugged and smiled, offering him a second length of twine like a person offering someone a rope across a creek.

"Here," she said. "Opposite end."

He took it, moved to the other chair, and the two of them lifted. Lanterns rose between them like a quiet constellation. Through the archway, the bakery smelled like apples and cinnamon and butter that had made its peace with destiny.

A small party of townsfolk wandered in and were promptly conscripted—Hank with his own chair ("I brought it from home. Government chairs wobble"), Tilly the mayor with a stack of sign-up sheets and a stance on extension cords ("absolutely no daisy chains; last year's sparks were memorable"), and Principal Moreno with an approving nod at Max's lettering. "Excellent spacing," she said. Max sat up so tall he nearly levitated.

Julian hid a grin and outlined another letter with ceremonial care.

"I like this one," Principal Moreno said, indicating APPLE SLICE STATION. "It implies impulse control."

"Lies," Ruth said cheerfully, refilling the cinnamon sugar. "We're a people of snacks."

The afternoon plumped around them: chatter, small decisions, the rattle of a jar of buttons, Agnes's low humming, Irene's soft cluck of approval when a bow landed just right. Twice, Julian felt that prickle again—cool air slipping under his collarbone, gone before he could squint at its origin. He blamed old windows and the way autumn sneaks into buildings that date back to the kind of carpentry people still brag about in old towns.

"Okay," Ruth called, clapping once. "Ten-minute break. Hydrate, and whatever you do, keep your glue sticks in your own lane."

Susan set a tray of cider on the counter. Nell did a quiet lap replacing spent tea lights with fresh ones and straightening a stack of paper. The candle flickered again; Beatrix had arrived— Mavis felt it as surely as she knew which cupboard held the good mugs.

"Posture," came a crisp voice only the Whitlocks heard. Beatrix slid up beside Ivy's shoulder, inspecting the FESTIVAL sign. "That S is sliding downhill. Give it a spine."

Ivy corrected it, unaware of the ghostly nod she received.

"Max," Beatrix added, "lanterns in threes. The eye prefers odd numbers. And your apostrophe on children's should curl, not stab."

"It was stabbing," Max admitted, fixing it.

Mavis felt laughter rise and decided she could save it for later, when Julian wasn't three feet away being exceptionally good at looking like a person who didn't notice drafts that moved with intention.

"Julian," Mavis said, "how's your moral authority?"

He held up HISTORICAL SCAVENGER HUNT—clean, confident, ready to pin. "Usable in court."

"Principal Moreno is sterner than a judge," Mavis said, accepting the sign. Their fingers brushed again; neither called it an accident.

He cleared his throat. "This—" he gestured gently, taking in the tables, the aunts, the bakery bustle, Max's earnest concentration, Ivy's precise capitals, Benji's buckled pumpkin— "is very good for the soul."

"That's in the charter, too," Mavis said softly.

He opened his mouth, then shut it. A thousand thoughts lined up; he chose one. "You look happy," he said. It was simple. It landed.

"I am," she said, and he gave her a smile that looked a lot like tenderness.

The last hour ran on laughter and small victories. Hank declared two garlands "structurally improbable." Lydia invented a ribbon system. Ruth rescued a table from a glue gun. Agnes and Irene debated bow sizes with the quiet intensity of diplomats. Principal Moreno found the sign-up slot for GUESS THE CANDY CORN and wrote Max's name in neat block letters. Max pretended he hadn't wanted that all afternoon. Benji added a tiny blue bell to the painted buckle ("for flair"), then asked if flair was legal ("within reason," said the mayor).

Twice, the front bell gave that content, single note it reserved for known souls. Nibs, the glossy black cat with eyes like copper buttons, sauntered in, inspected a coil of twine, and vanished between table legs without allowing petting. Julian watched him go, mystified. "Does he live here?"

"He lives where he pleases," Mavis said.

"An independent voter," Julian said gravely.

"Swing district," Ruth murmured, and the table dissolved into laughter again.

As the sun slipped toward honey, they strung the last lanterns on a test line between the archway and a tall bookcase. Julian steadied the chair while Mavis reached, the jute in her hands, the lanterns brushing her knuckles like patient planets.

When she stepped down, she was close enough that he could see the faint ink smudge on her ring finger, the little crescent D-shaped nick at the base of her thumb from a lifetime of box cutters and book corners.

"Thank you," she said, not just for the chair.

"My pleasure," he said, not just for the lanterns.

The room did that small softening again; then Agnes clapped once and the spell shattered cheerfully into brooms and sweeping assignments.

"Max, Ivy—floor. Benji, table glitter. Everyone else: chairs and string containment," Irene directed, tea towel over one shoulder like a general's sash.

Julian picked up a broom without being asked. "Civic duty," he announced, and swept glitter like a man who had never met it in the wild.

"You missed a spot," Benji said, helpful.

"Benji," Mavis said, equally helpful, "say 'thank you for sweeping, Julian.'"

Benji considered. "Thank you for sweeping, Julian. You missed a spot."

Julian laughed and swept the spot.

By the time the last garland was labeled and the glue guns unplugged with the solemnity they required, the light outside had gone pearly. The lanterns glowed softly along the ceiling, making their own kind of atmosphere. Max leaned into Mavis's side, tired and triumphant. Ivy tucked the finished FESTIVAL banner under her arm like an heirloom. Benji jingled the tiny bell he'd painted on the pumpkin and declared it "road-safe."

"Day well spent," Lydia said, winding raffia into tidy halos.

"Festival will look like itself," Nell added, satisfaction in her voice.

Ruth pressed leftover cinnamon knots into a paper bag and shoved it at Julian. "For walking-home fortitude."

"Your policies are very generous," he said.

"I'm easily impressed by people who sweep," she said.

He glanced at Nell. "Walk you to the inn?"

Nell nodded, "The kids and Peter should be finished setting up over there by now, we can grab them on our way."

Julian zipped up, saluted Ruth with a crumb-dusted dignity, and Nell hugged Irene and Agnes with the kind of care you use when you know you're hugging your history.

At the door, another faint brush of cool air passed Julian's cheek, and he felt, unmistakably, approval; two parts Beatrix, one part Hattie, a pinch of Sybil.

Outside, the street had softened into evening. Lantern tests glowed through the front windows like a promise. Julian adjusted the paper bag in his hand, fell into step beside Nell, and exhaled like a man who'd only just realized he'd been holding his breath.

"Feels like a town getting ready for something it loves," he said.

"It is," Nell said, and when she looked up at him, the thought came unbidden and easy: Maybe he is, too.

They walked on—past the lamppost that always flickered once for known souls, past the chalkboard that would, later tonight, write tomorrow's knittery schedules in Irene's hand without Irene's hands. Nell chattered about booth shifts. Julian promised to be there early.

Behind them, back inside the bookshop, the tea lights puffed out with a wink of Agnes's eye as if pleased with the day's work.

Chapter Seventeen

By the time the first red leaves clung to the gutters along
Maplewick's main street, the Autumn Festival was no longer just
an item on the town meeting agenda—it was everywhere. The
square smelled faintly of cinnamon and woodsmoke. Shop
windows were dressed in cornstalks and pumpkins. Lists were
being made on every available scrap of paper: booth schedules,
supply runs, last-minute decorations.

For Mavis, the beginning of September had been a blur of
bookshop hours, retreat prep, and time with Julian. Somehow,
the last part had folded itself into her life without feeling like an
interruption—just... an addition. They'd spent afternoons
walking the ridge trail and evenings bent over maps or old
ledgers at the bookshop table, mugs of coffee and tea between
them.

Julian had come and gone a few times, day traveling to other
New England towns for his article. Each evening, he returned to
the Maplewick Inn, where Nell had quietly kept his room
waiting. It had begun to feel natural for Mavis to see him stroll
across the square in the mornings, or to find him already at work
at the back table when she came downstairs from the apartment;
Susan having let him in from the bakery side.

Her family had noticed, of course. Ruth teased her. Max, after an initial curiosity, had settled into treating Julian like part of the furniture—albeit the kind who could be roped into helping with homework, candy corn guessing practice, or sneaking cinnamon buns from next door. Even Nell's husband, Owen, had started greeting Julian with the kind of nod reserved for people who'd proven themselves trustworthy.

It was a strange, steady kind of happiness, Mavis thought— one that didn't shout, but hummed along. And as the festival crept closer, she found herself looking forward to the day with more than her usual fondness for autumn.

ᴕ ᴕ ᴕ

One evening, Julian showed up at the bookshop just before closing, the September light already low enough to gild the dust motes. He leaned on the counter like a man who'd been carrying around a secret all day and was finally ready to let it out.

"You busy tonight?" he asked.

Mavis looked up from her ledger. "That depends."

"On what?"

"On whether 'busy' means staying here to do inventory or...?"

"Or packing a picnic and coming with me to the Mill at dusk," he said, leaning in just enough for her to catch the cedar-and-paper scent of him. "Let's go see if we can catch the ghost of the worker humming."

She arched a brow. "Ghost-hunting on a school night?"

He smiled, slow and warm. "I'm thinking less hunting, more... listening. And maybe—" His voice dipped, almost conspiratorial. "—seeing what else we find."

Before she could answer, the connecting door from the bakery swung open and Ruth breezed in, a flour-dusted apron tied at her waist. "What's this I hear about the Mill?" she asked, eyes darting between them.

"Nothing," Mavis said quickly.

"Something," Julian countered, not breaking eye contact with Mavis. "I'm asking her to come back to the mill with me tonight."

Ruth grinned like a cat in cream. "Well, well. In that case Max can sleep over. The kids will love it. And you," she pointed a scone at Mavis, "can go chase ghosts or... whatever."

Mavis gave her sister a look, but Ruth was already backing toward the bakery, mouthing you're welcome before disappearing.

The Mill lay quiet under the dusky sky, the air cool enough to prickle her skin. Julian had spread a blanket near the water, the low rush of it just audible over the sound of crickets. He unpacked bread that was still warm from the inn's oven, sharp cheese, apples, and a flask of tea.

They ate in companionable quiet until the last of the light began to slide away. Then Julian shifted closer, his knee brushing hers. "I wasn't completely honest," he murmured.

Mavis tilted her head. "About what?"

"This," he said, his gaze fixed on her mouth. "I wanted an excuse to get you here. Alone. No clocks, no interruptions."

Her pulse jumped. "And the ghost?"

"Still a bonus," he said, but his voice was rougher now.

He reached for her hand, not tentative this time, his fingers curling around hers before pulling her toward him. The kiss came with no hesitation—warm, sure, tasting faintly of apples and tea. She leaned into it, her hand sliding to the back of his neck, feeling the solid heat of him beneath his shirt.

Julian deepened the kiss, his other hand bracing on the blanket as if he wanted to pull her closer but was still holding back. She could feel the restraint in him, like a coiled wire, and it made her want to push, just a little.

When they broke apart, they were both breathing harder, foreheads still touching.

"I haven't felt pulled to someone like this in... a very long time," he said quietly, his thumb brushing the edge of her jaw.

Mavis swallowed, her voice low. "I haven't wanted someone this much in a very long time either," she admitted.

The air between them felt electric, threaded with all the things they hadn't yet said. The Mill stood silent behind them, the water carrying their breaths away into the dark.

They stayed like that for a moment, letting the quiet press around them. Somewhere in the trees, a night bird called, and the water moved steadily on.

Mavis leaned back just enough to look at him. "You know, Max is staying at Ruth's tonight." She reminded him.

Julian's eyes searched hers, the corners of his mouth curving just slightly. "Is that so?"

She nodded, her pulse thudding in her throat. "Which means the apartment will be... very quiet."

There was a beat where neither of them moved, and then she added, softer, "If you wanted to... come by."

Julian's expression shifted to something warm, like he'd been hoping she'd say it but didn't want to press. "I'd like that," he said simply, the words carrying more weight than they seemed to on the surface.

Her heart gave a little kick. "We should probably pack up before the ghost decides to join us."

He laughed under his breath and only let go of her hand to gather the blanket and the remains of their picnic. The path back toward town was lit in patches by the rising moon, and though they didn't speak much, the air between them was charged in a way that made Mavis acutely aware of every brush of his arm against hers.

❧ ❧ ❧

The shop was dark when they reached it, the square hushed under the glow of lamplight. Mavis unlocked the front door, and as soon as it clicked shut behind them, Julian stepped in close enough that the air shifted between them.

"Still quiet upstairs?" he asked, his voice low.

She swallowed, feeling her pulse quicken. "Still quiet."

Before she could take a step, his hand slid to her waist, guiding her back until her shoulders brushed the familiar wood of the shelves. The scent of him, cool night air, woodsmoke, and the bookshop, warm and familiar, curled around her. When he kissed her, there was nothing tentative about it. It was deep, certain, as though the hours at the mill had been a slow-burning fuse and this was the moment it finally caught.

Her fingers gripped the lapels of his coat, pulling him closer. The faint creak of the floorboards seemed too loud in the quiet shop. He kissed her again, slower, his thumb brushing her jaw as if memorizing it.

They didn't speak as they crossed the shop, still holding hands, pausing at the counter where her fingertips grazed the edge before he tugged her gently toward the stairs. Each step felt deliberate, like they were both acutely aware of what they were choosing.

Upstairs, the apartment welcomed them with the soft glow of a lamp and the comforting scent of home. Mavis barely set her keys in the dish before Julian's arm was around her again, pulling her in.

"I've been wanting this since the first time I saw you," he murmured against her temple.

Her breath caught. "And now?"

"Now I'm wondering how I'm supposed to leave," he said, his mouth finding hers again.

The kiss deepened, her back meeting the wall, his hands warm at her hips. She felt the steady thud of his heartbeat under her palms as she pressed closer. The world narrowed to the weight of his touch, the way his breath mixed with hers.

They made their way toward the couch by the window, never fully breaking contact—her hand brushing the side of his neck, his fingers trailing along her arm. They sank into the cushions, bodies angled toward each other, and the next kiss was slower but charged, full of the unspoken promise that neither of them wanted the night to end.

His thumb brushed the inside of her wrist, a quiet, grounding touch that somehow made her heart race more. He looked at her like he was memorizing her, like every second mattered.

The square outside was hushed, the lamplight glinting off the glass, but inside, the air between them was alive; warm, urgent, and pulling them both toward something they hadn't dared name until now.

Julian's hand threaded into her hair, tilting her head just enough for him to kiss her again—slower this time, but with a weight that made her pulse thrum. She felt the world outside the window fade, leaving only the warmth of his body pressed to hers and the quiet rush of their breathing.

Her fingers slid from the collar of his coat to the soft wool of his sweater, feeling the shape of his shoulders beneath it. He pulled back just enough to look at her, and she saw it—desire, yes, but also something steadier, deeper, as though he was already choosing her.

"Tell me if you want me to stop," he murmured.

She shook her head, her voice barely above a whisper. "Don't stop."

That seemed to undo him. He pulled off their coats and drew her closer, the space between them vanishing. His mouth found hers again, his kiss warm and sure, the scrape of his stubble a sweet burn against her skin. She felt the slide of his palm along her side, stopping just at her ribs, his thumb stroking lightly through the fabric of her sweater.

When she shifted, his hand caught hers, their fingers threading together. He guided her back until she was leaning into the corner of the couch, and he hovered over her just enough that she could feel the solid line of him without any part of it feeling rushed.

She studied his face in the lamplight—how his lashes cast shadows against his cheek, the curve of his mouth when he wasn't smiling, the faint scar at the edge of his jaw that she hadn't noticed before. She wanted to trace all of it with her fingertips.

"I haven't felt pulled to someone like this in years," he admitted, voice low and almost rough.

Her chest tightened, heat blooming low and deep. "Me neither."

He kissed her again, and this time there was nothing slow about it. It was a kiss that spoke of everything unsaid between them, of nights apart and glances across rooms, of the weeks that had been building to this. She answered with the same urgency, her hands slipping beneath the edge of his sweater, finding warm skin and the steady flex of muscle beneath her fingertips.

His breath caught, and he smiled against her lips before kissing her again, softer now, his forehead resting against hers. They stayed like that for a long moment—breathing each other in, neither moving away.

When they finally pulled back, it was only enough for her to curl into his side, his arm wrapping around her like it belonged there. Outside, the square was hushed, the last lamplight having faded into the deeper dark of night.

And in that quiet moment, Mavis knew she didn't want him to leave. Not tonight.

Chapter Eighteen

The next morning, Julian took his coffee onto the inn's side porch, where the thick ivy climbed the railings. The square was doing that late-September thing—cool shade pooled under the elms, sunlight was golden along the storefronts, someone testing a strand of paper lanterns and pretending it wasn't because they were impatient for October.

His phone buzzed. Elena Park.

He stared at the screen long enough to invent three excuses and a new personality, then answered. "Hey."

"Hey yourself," said his editor, brisk and not unkind. "How's Maplewick? Do they believe in commas?"

"Passionately," he said, smiling despite himself.

"Good. Because production believes in deadlines. I love the photos you sent, and the Portsmouth draft needs to move from your notes to my inbox by the tenth. Then Salem. Then Rockport. We'll schedule you a week in each—tourism boards are being extremely accommodating and the hotel deals expire.

Julian pinched the bridge of his nose. A wrought-iron chair creaked somewhere. "Elena, what if we rearranged? Kept Maplewick as the anchor? I can file a piece from here this week and—"

"You're charming and stalling," she said, and he could hear typing on her end. "I know the game, Everett. You fall for a town. You want to be thorough. I love that for your research, but we have six features to deliver and two pages of ad copy with pumpkins on them waiting for your captions."

He looked out at the square, where Agnes and Irene crossed with a basket of knitted bunting like a winged creature between them. "I promised people I'd—" he began, then stopped. He couldn't tell his editor he'd promised a ten-year-old he'd run a candy-corn booth.

"Promised who?" Elena asked, tone softening just a fraction.

"Myself," he said, and hated how limp it sounded. "Promised myself I'd do this right. That I would take my time and be thorough."

A beat; a sigh. "Julian. You are doing it right. But we don't have the budget for sentimentality. We have trains, ferries, a photographer who wears a beret unironically, and a layout schedule. I need you in Portsmouth by the end of next week. Two days to pack, move, settle. Can you live with that?"

He thought of lanterns drying on a line in the bookshop, of Max's neat block letters on a poster board, of Mavis's small, private laugh when a joke landed exactly right. His chest tightened.

"I can do it," he said finally. "I'll get you copy from here today. And I'll," He swallowed. "I'll head out."

"Text me your ETA," Elena said, efficient again. "And hey—don't make that voice. You can go back. Just not this month."

"Right," he said.

They hung up. The wind lifted once, cool across his collar. He stared at the phone like it had misbehaved. When he looked up, Nell was in the doorway with a basket of folded napkins and the kind of face you make when you're deciding whether to ask.

"Everything alright?" she said gently.

He arranged his mouth into something calm. "Deadline pep talk."

Nell's smile held more understanding than he wanted to deal with. "We put extra cinnamon in the lobby coffee," she said. "Emergency provision."

"Civilized," he said, and meant thank you.

"Civilization is my brand," she said, then left him to his wrestle.

He took a breath, then another, and did what he always did when his mind threatened to spin: he fetched his notebook and walked toward the one place that had begun to quiet the noise in his head and calm his heart.

⁊❧ ⁊❧ ⁊❧

The bell at Whitlock Books often announced the good people in a tone Mavis knew was different from the stranger ring. Today, it didn't ring at all.

Julian stepped over the threshold and hesitated. Mavis's back was to him at the counter, head tipped toward Max, who sat on a stool hugging his knees. The shop had that late-afternoon hush, the kind that made you aware of your own footsteps. He didn't want to crack it.

"—he'll be there, right?" Max's voice was low, the kind he used when he wanted to sound casual and forgot he was ten. "For the festival, I mean. He said he would."

Mavis's hands were steady; her voice, steadier. "He said he would," she said.

Max considered this, then kicked the rung of the stool once, soft. "Is that like—" He swallowed. "Like when my dad left? Did *he* say he'd stay with us?"

A crack, faint and precise, right down Julian's center.

Mavis leaned in, brushed hair off Max's forehead with the care of someone who knew every worry that lived there. "Not really," she answered truthfully. "That was different. But, that wasn't about us, that was about him. And we—" she tapped Max's wrist, light and certain "—we have a whole town and family who are here for us and love us. Not everyone has that." She pulled him into a hug and kissed the top of his cheek.

Max huffed a breath, which was as close as he got to hope when he was trying not to show it. "Okay," he said. "I just... like when people keep promises."

"As you should," she said. "Me too."

Julian stood there, a man-shaped apology in a doorway, while the bell had decided to let him in without calling attention to it, he cleared his throat quietly to announce his presence.

Mavis looked up. Surprise flickered, followed by something like relief, followed by a small, guarded tuck of her mouth that told him she was bracing for whatever came next.

"Hi," he said to both of them, gently. "I brought—" He lifted the tote, like evidence. "The Sanborn maps from the town

174

hall copier. The 1898 set. Thought we could figure the old mill road for part of the scavenger hunt."

Max slid off the stool with the dignity of a person who'd just been overheard feeling something. "I have to go help Aunt Ruth carry flour," he announced, which was news to everyone. "For my muscles." He paused, shot Julian a look that was half challenge, half invitation. "You coming to the festival early? I'm in charge of the jar."

"I am," Julian said, before he could puzzle out how. "I'll be there."

Max nodded like a foreman approving a subcontractor and disappeared through the archway, the bakery door swinging behind him.

Silence re-knit itself. Mavis exhaled, the tiniest thread of tension leaving her shoulders. "The bell likes you now," she said, not quite a question.

"I think it chose not to interrupt," he said. "I didn't mean to—"

"You were just there," she said, saving him from the apology. "It happens."

He set the tote on the counter and slid out the maps. "I got a call," he said. "From my editor."

"Ah," she said, and he could see her take the word and hold it carefully, like it might spill scalding water.

"They want me in Portsmouth by the end of next week," he said. "Salem after that. Rockport. They have hotel blocks and photographers with berets and... a schedule they want to keep."

"Photographers with berets," she repeated, dry smile ghosting across her mouth. "A formidable force."

"I told her I wanted to stay through the festival," he said. "I promised—" He swallowed. "I promised Max I'd help with his booth. I told him I'd be there early to set up."

Her eyes flicked to his, then away. "And will you?"

The simplest question he'd heard in months, and it had an edge that made him hate himself a little for not being able to answer with the single syllable both of them deserved.

"I'm trying to negotiate," he said. "I don't know if I'll win."

She nodded once, as if she'd prepared for this answer since the day he walked into her shop. "Jobs are jobs," she said, not unkindly. "They ask for things at inconvenient times."

"I don't want to be another person who leaves you two," he said, too bare, too fast. "I don't... I know that story. I don't want it."

Her face changed by a degree you'd miss if you weren't watching her closely. Something softened; something also stepped back a half-inch. "I appreciate that," she said, and meant it. "But you're allowed to have a life that isn't arranged around our old wounds."

He flinched, not because she'd hurt him but because she was right. "I'm sorry," he said. "That was selfishly phrased."

She studied him for a beat, then tapped the corner of the top map and lifted it open. "Show me the mill road," she said gently. "Before we re-pave it with hypotheticals."

He let out a breath he hadn't realized he'd been holding and leaned in. The paper smelled like old linen, the kind repositories keep—years pressed flat by care. It was familiar and comforting at that moment. Their shoulders almost touched; the map spanned the counter like a treaty.

"Here," he said, tracing the faint line south of the river. "The 1898 sheet labels an outbuilding. Sheds, maybe. If the scavenger hunt sends people past the low wall, you could chalk arrows that—"

Mavis reached for a pencil at the same moment he did. Their fingers bumped; hers were ink-smudged, his warm. Neither pulled away as quickly as they could have.

"The chalk will write itself if we ask nicely," she said, deadpan.

He huffed a small laugh, grateful for it. "I'm starting to believe that's not a metaphor."

"It's Maplewick," she smiled. "You never know."

They worked in a companionable quiet. Each holding space for each other's thoughts while trying to hold of sadness. He felt the steadiness of her in the way she chose routes—clear, practical, forgiving of detours. He showed her how to layer the vellum so the old road lined up with the current one. She showed him, with the ball of her thumb, how to press the edge so the curl stayed flat.

At some point their heads drew closer; at some point the map ceased to be between them. He looked up and found her looking back, and the room tilted, just slightly, toward the thing neither of them wanted to rush but neither of them would deny.

"Julian," she said, quiet.

"I know," he said, just as quiet.

He leaned in and she met him. The kiss was careful and present and warmer than he deserved on a day he had brought a problem to her door. When they parted, her hand stayed where it was—light on the map's margin, close to his.

"If I stay," he said, "if I stay—" He tried again. "If I figured out a way to make Maplewick home base—travel for work, write from here—would there be... anything for me to stay for? With you?"

It was not slick. It was not rehearsed. It was just his heart on his sleeve.

Her eyes dipped; she let the question land and sit a breath. When she looked up, she wasn't coy. She wasn't careless either.

"There's already something," she said. "But I can't make your choices for you. I won't. I have Max to think about. And myself." The corners of her mouth lifted, small and real. "If you stay because you chose it, not because you were cornered, we'll see what we can build from what we already have."

He nodded and gave a sad smile. "Fair," he said. "Good. Right."

From the bakery came the thump of a sack of flour landing on the prep table and Max's voice announcing, "Muscles acquired." The bell gave a single pleased note—someone known—and the afternoon remembered itself.

Julian rolled the maps with care. "I should let you work," he said. "And I should go file a story about a town that is not going to let me leave without making me say please."

"Go write," she said, and the softness in it undid him a little more. "And Julian—"

He looked up.

"Thank you for asking the question out loud," she said. "Not everyone does."

He managed a smile and hesitated. "Tell Max I'll try to be at his booth. Early. Even if it's only to help set up before—" He didn't finish. He didn't have to.

She nodded. "I'll tell him." She wouldn't, she couldn't make a promise that she wasn't sure would be kept. She would pick up the pieces like she always did, not matter what.

He stepped backward toward the door, unwilling to turn his back for the two steps it took to leave. The lamppost outside flickered once when he opened it—the little nod it gave to those the town had started to count as it's own. He felt it and tried, for once, not to overexplain it to himself.

꙰ ꙰ ꙰

He packed like a man who wanted to be argued with by his own suitcase.

At the inn, he laid shirts in neat stacks and then unstacked them. He put his notebook in the satchel, then took it back out and set it on the desk as though it might anchor him by sheer intimacy with the wood. He opened the laptop and wrote Elena an email he didn't send:

I can give you Portsmouth. I can give you Salem. But I'll give them to you from Maplewick. I'm planting roots because it's about time I do.

He stared at the blinking cursor. He thought about the way Max had said the word 'promise.' He thought about a shop bell that chose not to tattle, about a map that smelled like linen, about a woman who answered questions with her whole face.

He closed the laptop without saving. Outside his window, the square carried on—someone testing a banjo phrase, someone else scolding a glitter jar. The lamplight hadn't come on yet; it would, soon. He imagined, absurdly, that the town watched from the corners and took notes.

"Two days," he said into the empty room. "Work fast."

He sat. He pulled his laptop and notebook closer. He began to write the Maplewick piece with a sentence he hadn't intended:

Some towns are where you go to visit the past; some are where your past politely pulls out a chair and asks whether you plan to stay.

He didn't know yet if he would. But for the first time in a long time, his life and the writing lined up.

He kept going.

Chapter Nineteen

By morning, Maplewick had put on its gilt-edged September
face—crisp air, warm sun across the shingles and a sense of
getting-on-with-it that made even the pigeons look industrious.
Mavis propped the bookshop door with the wooden fox and
chalked a quick FESTIVAL HELPERS NEEDED across the
sidewalk slate. The shop smelled like lemon oil and last night's
tea. Hattie had lined three lanterns along the front table; their
glass panes winked.

Max barreled down the apartment stairs at the speed of a
boy who'd remembered there were glue sticks downstairs. "Aunt
Ruth said I can make the Guess-the-Candy-Corn sign if I don't
go too heavy with the glue."

"A reasonable boundary," Mavis said, straightening the stack
of poster board.

He peered at her, the too-knowing gaze he'd inherited from
every Whitlock woman. "You look like a person who has
something on her mind."

"Nah, just something in my hand... a cup of tea," she countered.

He accepted this gravely, then leaned on the counter. "Do you think Julian's gonna help with the jar? I was thinking we could make it hard. Like not a boring number."

"I think," Mavis said carefully, "that Julian is trying his best to be everywhere at once. Sometimes grown-ups can't."

Max made a face and pressed two palms to the glass candy jar like he could summon it full by love. "I'm still making it complicated," he said. "With twizzlers."

"Your cleverness is noted," she said, and kissed the crown of his head.

The bell gave a short, familiar note and Julian stepped in with a roll of butcher paper under one arm and the guilty look of a man who'd brought offerings because he didn't know how to bring news.

"Ambassador," Mavis said lightly.

"Cartographer," he returned, lifting the paper. "Festival maps. Street closures, booth numbers, a friendly arrow that says COOKIES."

"Public service."

Max popped up like a meerkat. "Are you coming early to help level the candy corn? Mom says it can't be rigged."

"I said it shouldn't be rigged," Mavis corrected, because accuracy mattered.

Julian smiled at Max, and something in it pinched Mavis's heart just enough to feel. "I want to," he said. "I—" He glanced at Mavis, then back to the boy. "I have some not-so-great news. It's looking like I have to hop on to Portsmouth for work. But I'm working on it. If I can, I'll be there. Early."

Max nodded like a tiny accountant doing math. "Oh, okay," he whispered.

"Okay," Julian said softly.

Ruth's head appeared in the bakery doorway, pencil stabbed into the messy bun in her hair, apron already flour-dusted. "Who authorized this meeting without snacks?" she demanded. "Here, taste test." She slid over a plate of maple twists, then gave Julian a look that saw through four layers of his composed face. "You've got worry on your face," she said. "Is it the fixable kind or the kind where you need carbs?"

"Both probably," he admitted.

"Good," Ruth said. "Eat, then lift this flour for me so Max has role models."

Max puffed his chest. "Muscles."

"Exactly."

For ten minutes the room pretended nothing hurt. They tasted icing and argued about whether the lantern walk should start at the church or the inn. Max drew a truly villainous candy corn with eyebrows. Mavis laughed and it wasn't fake; it just fell a little flat.

When the plate was down to sugar crumbs, Julian wiped his hands, set the roll of paper by the counter, and found Mavis's gaze. "Walk?" he asked, a word that fit more weight than the letters could carry.

"Two blocks," she said. "Max, would you go check if Aunt Ruth needs any more help?"

Max, busy shading a menacing triangle, waved them away with benevolent authority. "I'll be in the bakery using my muscles responsibly."

After watching Max step through the door to her sister, Mavis stepped out into the mild light to meet Julian where he waited in front of the shop. Across the square, Agnes and Irene were directing other townsfolk with the stringing of knitted garlands between lampposts, a rainbow of stitches looping like a spell. Agnes saw them, tipped her head in greeting, and then, because she could, sent a leaf-skitter of breeze that made the bunting hum like a pleased cat. Irene lifted two fingers at them—the smallest benediction.

Julian watched the aunties with open fondness. "Your family runs this place," he said.

"Ha," Mavis smiled slightly. "Sometimes it sure seems like it."

They walked the inner loop of the square, where chalk ghosts already grinned in front of the general store and Hearth & Bloom had a bucket of cattails posed like fireworks. Nibs, the black cat, sat prim as punctuation on the knittery steps and blinked once like a judge.

"I don't know how to do this without messing it up," Julian said finally, words small and careful. "My editor wants me on a train. I want to be two places. I haven't managed that yet in my life."

Mavis tucked her hands into her cardigan sleeves. She didn't look at him; she looked out towards the churchyard where she knew curious souls were watching them. "I don't need guarantees," she said. "I need clarity. If you're going to go for a few days, go. If you can come back for the festival, come. Don't promise Max something you can't deliver."

"I won't," he said, and that was the truest thing he'd said all morning. "I'll tell him 'I'll try,' and I will mean it. I love my work, Mavis. I've never had to practice balancing my love of work with my love —" he paused realizing what he was about to say, "my pull towards anything else. I want to do my job well, I *need* to do my job well, but I also want you to know how much I want to do this well too. I'll be hounding that return train schedule like a wolf."

She smiled then, faint but real—amusement on her face. "A wolf huh?"

"Academic wolf," he conceded. "The least frightening wolf."

They stopped at the church steps, where the bell rope hung like a secret. He turned to her. "Last night, after I wrote for a while, I kept thinking about your 'already something,'" he said. "I don't want to press that into a shape it isn't ready to be."

"It already has a shape," she said. "We just haven't named it yet." She met his eyes. "You're doing the right thing, telling me instead of sneaking out at dawn and leaving a clever note."

"I had three drafts of clever notes," he joked.

"Very funny." she admonished, and the corner of her mouth lifted.

They stood there in a pocket of uncomplicated honesty until the wind shifted and the smell of cinnamon said the bakery had pulled another tray.

"I should pack," he said. "And file."

"Go pack," she said. "I'll be here, bullying twine."

He bent, kissed her once, brief and firm, a promise of a promise he couldn't make out loud. When he straightened, there was a look on his face that made her want to both follow him and push him away. She did neither. She let him go.

Nibs rose, stretched like a sentence, and trotted after him to the corner before vanishing under a parked truck, news of their conversation tucked into his mind.

꒰ ꒰ ꒰

The day did what days do: kept going.

By noon, the homework table had morphed into a crafting headquarters. Ivy sorted ribbon by a system known only to her and God. Benji lobbied for a bat puppet that would "swoop respectfully." Max, tongue caught between teeth in concentration, printed RULES in bubble letters that looked like they might run for office.

Hattie, always on hand when needed, floated a clean pair of scissors exactly when Mavis reached for them, which was love in a language their family had always spoken.

"Mom?" Max asked, not looking up. "If Julian can't come, can Uncle Owen help me level the jar? He's fair. He says 'hmm' a lot."

"He's very judicious," Mavis agreed. The yes sat under her tongue. "We'll make sure you have help."

Max nodded, reassured by a back-up plan.

By afternoon, Agnes appeared with a basket of knitted leaves that somehow smelled faintly of rosemary. Irene stole the chalkboard and wrote CANDY CORN: GUESS WITHOUT CHEATING in her beautiful, bossy hand. Lydia popped in to drop off "nerve tonic" that tasted suspiciously like apple cider with extra clove. The knittery windows glowed with afternoon praise. The town warmed its hands at itself.

Mavis kept moving. Kept smiling. Kept the stitches even. She was good at that—making the day hold even when the weft tried to loosen.

Only once did she go still. It was when she found the 1898 map rolled tight where she'd left it with Julian. She slid it into the glass case with the ledger he'd brought from the inn and closed the latch with a click that sounded a little like a heart breaking.

"You're brooding," Ruth observed, appearing with sugar on her cheek.

"I'm arranging," Mavis said.

"Mm." Ruth tilted her head. "Those things sometimes wear each other's clothes."

Mavis huffed a laugh. "He's leaving tonight."

"For a bit," Ruth said. "Not forever." She bumped Mavis's shoulder with her own. "And if he is foolish enough to try forever, Agnes and I will simply redirect the trains."

"You can't redirect trains," Mavis said.

Ruth's smile was all teeth. "Can't we?"

In the far aisle, a book hopped half an inch and resettled as if to agree. Mavis exhaled, her squeezed chest loosening, purely because her sister had said something ridiculous and meant it. She knew she was loved, even if Julian's enchantment with Maplewick, and her, faded with miles of distance between them.

᠅ ᠅ ᠅

He didn't sneak out at dawn. He left at dusk.

Just as the square tipped toward evening, when the lamps threw their first soft halos and the church bell considered being sentimental, Julian crossed the porch of the inn with a small suitcase, a satchel, and the look of a person who was being ripped in two directions at once.

Nell stood on the porch with a wrapped sandwich and a thermos that smelled like home. "Room's held," she said. "I put your book on the nightstand. The one you don't admit you're reading."

"Thank you," he said, throat tight.

"Go do the thing," she said. "Then come do this thing."

He nodded, took the sandwich, and held back from trying to pour a paragraph into the space where a simple goodbye belonged. He glanced across the square. The bookshop windows were lamplight and shadow; he could picture Mavis exactly— hair pinned up and escaping anyway, pencil behind her ear, the line between her brows when she was counting more than numbers.

He didn't go in. He didn't think he could leave if he put his hand on that counter. He lifted two fingers toward the windows in a private salute, and then he went.

A train whistle miles off sounded like someone else's story starting.

Night settled with its usual competence. The shop closed. The cousins texted logistics in a tornado of emojis. Max tried on his volunteer badge and practiced saying "Welcome to our extremely fair game" without giggling. Mavis washed three mugs by hand she could have put in the bakery's dishwasher because sometimes you needed the small ritual.

The apartment was very quiet when she climbed the last stair with a fresh mug of tea. She set her keys in the dish and stood a moment at the window. Down on the square, the lamppost nearest the knittery flickered once, then steadied. The knitted bunting shifted like a lake in a friendly breeze. Maplewick breathed.

She pressed her forehead to the cool glass, and the motion sent her tea steam curling into the shape of a heart before it unraveled—a silly, soft little gesture, like the house was trying to distract her with parlor tricks.

"Show-off," she said, fond, to no one and to everything.

From the bookcase below came the faintest thump. Hattie, she knew, putting something back where it belonged. Tonight

Mavis was particularly grateful for the help. She wasn't in the mood to straighten and clean the space where she'd spent the last several weeks with Julian now that he was leaving.

Mavis made her way to her bedroom and completed her bedtime routine. Then she turned off the lamp and crawled into bed and lay on her side where the mattress dipped just a little from years of just one side of the bed being slept on. She hurt, but she also felt alive in a way she hadn't let her life feel for a long time.

"Two days," she murmured into the dark, stealing the words he'd said. "Work fast."

Downstairs from the quiet shop, came a soft, calming sound—just a ghost humming to herself, hoping that everything would work out for her favorite girl.

Chapter Twenty

Some days moved like pins on a map—you could feel the line tugging between where you were and where you meant to be.

By breakfast, Maplewick had already started its festival hum. Someone across the square hammered something that wasn't urgent but sounded like it. The air tasted like apple peel and hope.

Max wolfed toast and inspected his volunteer badge as if it might try to escape. "We should practice leveling the jar," he announced. "Also I think we need a rule about no counting by handfuls."

"Strong governance," Mavis said, buttering another slice. Her phone buzzed on the counter, just once, then stilled. She didn't look at it. Not yet.

Max eyed her. "Is that Julian?"

"It might be," she said, honest.

"Do we want to know?"

"We do," she said, even more honest, and checked.

Julian: Missed the 2:19. Hoping to be ready for the 3:04. Not sure it connects.

Another buzz followed a few minutes later.

Julian: If I can't make the 3:04, the 3:37 gets me close, but it's tight.

Her thumb hovered, then typed back:

Mavis: Either way, safe travels.

Max read over her shoulder, lips pressing together. "He's still trying."

"He is," Mavis said. She kissed the crown of his head. "And that matters."

They left the apartment into a day that had dressed itself properly: blue sky with a few decorous clouds, breeze polite enough to lift the knitted bunting but not enough to knock over the mums. The bell approved of them with a single bright note. Hattie had already nudged the front table a half inch left, which made the room exhale. Beatrix's favorite dictionary lay askew on the homework table like a cat pretending it hadn't been caught napping.

By ten, the bookshop had become a mild chaos of purpose. Ruth leaned in with a sheet of stickers that said *I Guessed Honestly*, and stole a hug on the way out. Susan followed with a clipboard and an air of benevolent law. Owen walked past with two sawhorses; Nell followed with burlap runners; Lydia popped in with three tiny corked bottles "for nerves," which smelled suspiciously like chocolate milk. Agnes and Irene breezed through like weather, trailed by the scent of wool and rosemary.

"Forecast has opinions," Irene reported, hands on hips as she surveyed the square through the window.

"Kind ones?" Mavis asked.

Agnes flicked two fingers skyward, so small you'd miss it if you weren't built to notice. "We asked nicely," she said. "The clouds agreed—they can never say no to me." She winked.

Max arranged the candy corn jar, then rearranged, then crouched so his eye line was level with the meniscus of sugar. "No air pockets," he muttered like a surgeon. "Air is cheating."

"Strong science," Owen said solemnly. He had popped in hefting a sack of sand for the base of the booth. "You need me tomorrow?"

Max hesitated. "Maybe. If—" He didn't finish. He didn't have to. Owen squeezed his shoulder once, all promise and no pressure.

By noon, the chalkboard sign—CANDY CORN: GUESS WITHOUT CHEATING—had sprouted a tiny hand-drawn gavel courtesy of Ivy. Benji had contributed a bat with the polite label: swoops respectfully. Hattie aligned the stack of entry slips and, for flourish, set a tiny glass pumpkin beside the jar; the marigolds on the counter blushed a shade brighter as if to approve. The booth decor was almost ready.

The day tugged forward. Mavis set down twine and took it up again. She cut ribbon, counted paper cups, wrote *Welcome!* in her round hand until the word felt like a mantra. Every so often her phone buzzed, polite but increasingly guilty:

Julian: The 3:04 is not going to happen. :(

Julian: The 3:37 is delayed anyway. Would have missed the connection even if I could have gotten to the first train.

Julian: If I can't make it tonight, I'll try dawn. Don't hold the booth. Promise I'll try.

Each time she answered with small things that meant large ones:

Mavis: We'll be here.
Mavis: Max is practicing fairness doctrine.

At four, bad reception had swallowed his signal whole and spat back silence. The quiet landed on Mavis's shoulders like a shawl with a little too much weight.

"Tea," Lydia said, pressing a warm mug into her hands with the authority of a field medic. "And breathe *in* the steam, love. Not just at it."

Mavis breathed. The steam curled itself into a swirl and unraveled, soothing her nerves.

Work stitched the hours together. After school, Ivy and Benji arrived with pockets full of glitter and righteous intention. Max practiced his welcome. The cousins' group chat detonated twice with debates about extension cords and whether the banjo trio should be given a curfew. Nell floated through with a seating map and the rare, pleased glow of a woman whose lists had bent to her will.

"Tomorrow's going to be lovely," she said. "We have exactly four hay bales per booth, which is the correct number. I don't know why, but I feel that in my spirit."

"Your spirit is rarely wrong," Mavis said, and wished it so.

Twilight came on like a good story—line by line, without fuss. The square peppered with lanterns; the knitted bunting went soft as a river. People strolled the way people do when they're looking for each other and also for sizing up each other's booths. Hattie dimmed one lamp and brightened another until the shop wore its evening face. Nibs installed himself on the step outside and judged passersby benevolently.

Mavis stood at the window, phone in her pocket a quiet weight. The ache in her chest wasn't dramatic; it was practical. She could file it, even label it. *Wanting and progressive.* She was a woman who could feel two things at once: glad for what had been, aware of what might be lost.

"Brooding," Ruth diagnosed, appearing with a paper bag that smelled like cinnamon. "Prescribed: one apple-cider cruller and a hug."

Mavis accepted both. "Tell me again about redirecting the trains?" She said with a sad smile.

Ruth gave her sister a gentle look. "Aunt Agnes and mom did what they could about the weather. The rest is up to... train gods. And editors. And choices."

"Terrifying round-up," Mavis said, a laugh catching on the way out.

"Mm." Ruth tucked a stray curl behind Mavis's ear in a comforting, protective way. "Whatever happens, you've got us. And a small army of knitters who know where he stays when he's in town now."

"You are the very best."

"Undebatable," Ruth winked, and sashayed off to bully someone into taking extra crullers.

Evening settled. The lantern walk began; Nell at the front, Owen at her elbow, children bobbing with paper moons and stars, Agnes and Irene bringing up the rear like weather, Lydia distributing tiny paper cups of warm spiced cider. Mavis walked with Max, their shoulders bumping now and then, neither of them mentioning the space beside them that might yet be filled.

When the crowd circled back toward the square, the bell in the church tower offered a few, low, satisfied notes. People called their goodnights across the cobblestones. The bakery lights clicked to their comfortable dim. The bookshop gathered itself.

Max tugged Mavis's sleeve as they climbed the stairs to the apartment. "If he doesn't make it," he said, small but steady, "I'm okay with Uncle Owen. But... I still hope."

"Me too," she said, and kissed his hair.

They did the bedtime dance of teeth, pajamas, reading time, and one more sip of water. Max followed it with the sacred ritual of setting the volunteer badge beside the alarm clock. Max cozied into bed and tucked himself like a letter in an envelope.

"Want your door cracked?" Mavis asked.

"Medium," he said. "So the ghosts can check but not wake me up."

"I'll tell them," she promised. She turned off the light, left the door at an exacting halfway, and stood a moment in the hall breathing the small, good sounds of a boy going soft with sleep.

Her phone stayed quiet.

Downstairs, the shop's dark felt comfortable, not empty— shelves breathing, the faintest scent of peppermint and lemon hanging on. Mavis went to the counter and wrote herself a small note for morning: twine, slips, pencil cup, rule sign, candy. Her hand shook a little as she tucked the corner under the candy jar to keep it in place.

Behind her, a book eased itself out, then back, as if testing its hinge. "Not now," she told it gently. "We're fine."

Upstairs, she washed her face and brushed her hair and put on the softest nightshirt and did not cry. There was no use in rehearsing a sadness that might not arrive. She could meet it at the door if it did.

The square had settled to the sweet hush that only small towns can pull off; the hush that isn't empty but layered. Mavis set her phone on the windowsill and, on impulse, texted something she could live with no matter how the morning went.

Mavis: Don't forget to eat. Ruth says carbs make the trains run on time.

The three dots never blinked. She nodded once like a person making peace with something, and went to bed.

She dreamed of the mill's low humming—steady, sure, familiar—and a man walking toward her under knitted leaves. In the dream, she couldn't make out his face. She woke before he reached her.

Chapter Twenty-One

The day of the Autumn Festival had the kind of weather you'd order if you could. The sky was polished clear, air brisk enough for scarves and the sunlight was warm on the face. The square was already buzzing by mid-morning. Booths lined the cobblestones like a patchwork quilt: Lydia's table with jars of spiced cider syrup, Agnes and Irene's knitted bunting strung high across the lampposts, Ruth and Susan's bakery stall stacked with pies that vanished faster than they could cut them.

Mavis had stationed herself at Max's booth long enough to admire his handwritten RULES (bubble letters shaded aggressively) and his jar of candy corn, which had indeed ended up being made "complicated" by the inclusion of licorice whips and a lone caramel apple pop.

"Strategic chaos," Max explained, hands on hips.

"Creative sabotage," Ivy countered from the lantern crafts table.

Benji was simply trying to trade guesses for cookies.

The bell tower struck eleven and the music began. Fiddles, banjos, and the steady thump of a drum filled the air. People clapped along, laughing. Maplewick did this well: ordinary magic dressed as community spirit.

But Mavis felt the empty space anyway.

Every time she turned toward the bookshop, she half expected Julian to appear with his satchel and that slightly sheepish grin. Every time a tall man passed by, her chest gave a foolish little jump before settling back into the ache she'd been carrying since he left.

Max seemed to notice too, though he kept his chin up like a soldier. He leaned across the booth at one point and whispered, "It's fine that Uncle Owen is helping me. He keeps a soldier's eye on the jar."

Mavis smoothed his hair and kissed the crown of his head. "Yes," she said softly. "He's a good helper."

ॐ ॐ ॐ

The festival surged on—children with painted cheeks, the smell of cinnamon and fried dough, Agnes leading a sing-along she hadn't warned anyone about.

Mavis was at the cider booth when the air shifted. Not much, just a hush along her skin, like when a door opens behind you. She turned, and there he was.

Julian.

He was weaving through the crowd with a small suitcase trailing behind him, his satchel across his chest, and the look of a man determined. His hair was wind-tossed, his coat dusted with train grit, but his eyes—his eyes found hers across the square and didn't look away.

For a moment, she couldn't move. Then Max saw him.

"Julian!" Max hollered, vaulting the booth like a cat. He barreled into Julian with the force of all ten years of him, nearly toppling them both.

Julian bent, caught him tight, and laughed breathlessly against the boy's shoulder. "Hey, muscle man. Look at you, running an empire."

"You came back," Max said fiercely into his coat. "You said you'd try."

"I did," Julian said, his voice gentler now. He pulled back enough to meet Max's eyes, then pressed a hand to the boy's shoulder. "And I meant it."

Max beamed, radiant, then spun and sprinted toward the booth. "He's here! He's here!"

ॐ ॐ ॐ

That left Julian standing in the square, suitcase still by his side, looking straight at Mavis. She crossed the few steps before she could talk herself out of it.

"You came back," she said, the words tight in her throat.

"I did." He set the suitcase down next to him, like proof. His voice dipped low so only she could hear. "Because this—" his gaze flicked around them: the bunting, the children, the booths, then landed back on her—"this is where I want to be. With you. With Max. I missed home."

Her breath caught. "You're calling it home."

"I am," he said simply. "Because it is. The rest—the writing, the deadlines, the jobs—they'll fall into place. But this..." His hand brushed hers, tentative but sure. "This comes first now."

Her eyes burned, but she managed a shaky smile. "You realize you just said that in the middle of the square. Everyone is looking."

"Then I might as well finish what I started."

And before she could answer, before she could warn him about Whitlock gossip or the banjo trio's terrible timing, Julian kissed her. Right there, in front of the cider booth, under Agnes's knitted garlands, in full view of half the town. His hand cupped her cheek, warm and certain, and her fingers fisted in his coat like she'd been waiting her whole life to anchor him. The square went utterly still for one beat—then exhaled in a cheer that rippled like a wave.

Someone clapped. Someone else whooped. The fiddler struck up a jubilant reel without waiting for consensus.

Julian pulled back just enough to rest his forehead against hers, his grin unsteady and perfect. "Well," he said, loud enough this time, "I guess now everyone knows."

"About time!" Lydia hollered from her booth.

"Buy her a pie!" someone shouted.

Max stood on his bench, hands flung wide, yelling, "I told you he'd come!"

Mavis laughed through the sting of tears, kissed him again quick and certain, and let herself believe it: he was here. He was hers. And he was home.

The festival carried them forward—lanterns rising into the dusk, booths emptying their pies and crafts, children darting with sugared faces. But everywhere she turned, Julian was beside her. At Max's booth, leveling the jar with solemn precision. At the hayride, steadying her elbow as she climbed up beside the children. At the closing lantern walk, his fingers threading through hers like they'd been waiting for this exact moment.

Later, when the lanterns floated high above the square and the fiddles softened into something sweet, Mavis leaned against him and let herself believe what he'd said. That the rest would fall into place. That she, her son, the love she hadn't dared to want—came first.

Chapter Twenty-Two

The square wore its end-of-evening glow: lanterns still winking from the trees, booth tables half-collapsed like tired knees, a confetti of kettle-corn and ticket stubs skittering along the cobbles. Inside Ruth and Susan's cottage kitchen, the table sagged under teapots, pie slivers, and a scandalously lopsided candy-corn jar that Max had guarded like a dragon until the very end.

"Three hundred and eighty-seven," Max announced, chin up. "Not three hundred and eighty-eight like Ivy guessed. And not three hundred and eighty-five like Uncle Owen."

Ivy folded her arms, affronted in principle. "I was ONE off."

Benji, already frosting-adjacent, said gravely, "math problems."

From the doorway, Jonah, taller every time anyone looked at him, hair flopping into his eyes like it had opinions—lifted a brow. "So the jar is settled now?"

"It's about precision," Max said, delighted to have his teenage cousin care about his victory.

"Precision and integrity," Sophie added, solemn as a judge in jelly-bean pajamas.

Lillian, Nell's youngest, pushed up sparkly sleeves. "Can precision have frosting?"

"In this family?" Susan said, slipping a platter of cinnamon knots onto the table. "Definitely."

Lydia snorted. "Max was the closest. Agnes will be the final judge." Pawning off the argument to her mother.

"I will - Ivy wins and she will share the candy corn," Agnes decreed while untangling a skein of yarn like a woman who could out-maneuver Parliament before breakfast.

Julian, wedged between Nell and Mavis, leaned back and let it all sink in: the noisy comfort, the way conversation braided over itself, the stolen forkfuls of pie. He'd kissed Mavis in front of half the town, watched Max glow like a lantern at his booth, and now he sat in a kitchen that buzzed like a hive. He had no idea what more a man could reasonably want.

"Okay, sugar bugs," Ruth said at last, clapping once. "Upstairs. Teeth, pajamas, optional confessional about who smuggled a caramel apple under their coat."

"It wasn't me," Jonah said, which would have sounded convincing if Sophie and Lillian hadn't immediately chorused, "It was Jonah."

Max slid off his chair, the triumphant keeper of candy corn. "We're sleeping in the den," he told Julian. "We have a system. Jonah's in charge of flashlight politics."

"Very fair administration," Julian said gravely.

Jonah saluted with a flashlight already in hand. "Checks and balances."

The kid-parade thundered away, voices trailing up the stairs in a swirl of toothbrush negotiations and whispered conspiracies. Ruth and Susan exchanged the look of women who loved family chaos, then started stacking plates with the speed of veterans.

Susan pressed leftover knots into everyone's hands, as though carbs were a currency. Ruth kissed her sister's cheek, whispered something too fast to catch. The house sighed into its after-party quiet.

Lydia found her scarf draped over the back of a chair and muttered about it being borrowed without permission, which Peter swore he knew nothing about.

"Of course you don't," Lydia said, kissing his cheek anyway.

Owen turned to Mavis as he pulled on his jacket. "That boy of yours ran the candy-corn booth like a professional. Firm but fair. You should be proud."

"I am," Mavis said, smiling. "Though I think he'd rather you call it a 'jar of justice.'"

Peter chuckled. "Spoken like a true Whitlock."

One by one, the circle dissolved into the night. Owen ushered Agnes and Irene toward the square with the patience of a man who had done it before. Lydia tucked her arm through Peter's, the two of them vanishing into the soft glow of the lamplight. Nell called over her shoulder that Jonah would walk Max home in the morning as penance for the Carmel apple. Ruth and Susan waved from the stairs, already headed up to check on the progress of the children readying for their sleepover.

And then it was just Mavis and Julian standing in the warm-crumbed hush of the kitchen.

"I'll walk you home," Julian said, reaching for her coat before she could protest.

૭૪ ૭૪ ૭૪

Outside, the square was hushed. Lanterns still swayed on their strings, their flames guttering but stubborn. The knitted garlands across the lampposts moved faintly, though the air was mostly still. Nibs, the black cat, escorted them halfway across the cobblestones before disappearing beneath the library steps.

They walked slowly.

The night air was cool, edged with the scent of leftover hay bales. The square wore its after-festival face; ticket stubs skittering like confetti across the cobblestones, the booths packed down into shadows.

"You didn't have to," Mavis said quietly. "You must be tired."

"I wanted to," Julian replied.

They walked slow, shoes tapping the stones in companionable rhythm. Mavis tugged her cardigan tighter; Julian's hand brushed hers once, then again, until she let him catch it.

"This place," he said after a while, his voice low, "it already feels like it's mine. Like I missed home before I even admitted it was home."

She looked up at him, heart pressing against her ribs. "I like you calling it home," she said smiling, and her voice was soft but certain, as if the words themselves were a promise.

They reached the bookshop steps, the square still glowing with the last lanterns. Julian stopped, hands sliding over her shoulders, his eyes steady on hers.

"This is where I want to be," he said, his voice low and certain. "I've missed home before, but not like this. Not like you. I don't want to leave, Mavis. Not now, not ever."

She felt his words land inside her like a key turning. Before she could reply, he kissed her—hungry, unashamed, full of all the waiting they'd carried. Her fingers curled into his coat, holding him there until her knees nearly gave.

"You're mine now and everyone knows," she whispered when they finally parted, breathless.

"Good," Julian murmured, brushing his mouth along her jaw. "Let them know."

ೋ ೋ ೋ

Upstairs, the apartment glowed warm with lamplight. Mavis barely set her keys down before Julian pressed her gently back against the door, his kiss deeper now, his hands learning the shape of her as he'd meant to all along. She tugged him closer by his shirt, and his low laugh broke against her mouth before he kissed her again, harder.

"Julian," she breathed, her voice unsteady with want and wonder.

"I keep thinking I'll wake up and it won't be real," he said, his lips grazing her throat. "But it is. You are. And I don't want to waste another second pretending I don't want everything with you."

Her pulse fluttered at everything. She tipped his face back to hers, kissed him fiercely. "Good. Because I want everything too."

The rest of the night unraveled—kisses deepening as Julian's hands slid down her arms, as Mavis pulled him toward the bedroom with a certainty that surprised even her. The quilt was still turned down from earlier, lavender faint in the sheets. He laid her gently against them, pausing long enough to search her eyes for permission before he went further.

She answered with her hands in his hair, her mouth pulling him back down. Laughter flickered between them as sweaters tangled, then gave way to quiet, breathless sounds that belonged only to them. He moved with a reverence that undid her, tracing her like he was learning a language he'd been meant to speak all his life.

And she let herself lean into the wanting she'd carried for so long—into the steadiness of him, the surety, the warmth.

Later, when the room had gone hushed again and their breathing found the same rhythm, Mavis curled against him beneath the quilt, her cheek on his chest. The steady thud of his heart grounded her more than she wanted to admit.

"I didn't think I'd get this," she whispered into the quiet. "Not after Max's dad. Not after... everything."

Julian kissed the crown of her hair, his hand firm at her back. "You deserve this," he said, voice rough with certainty. "All of it. I don't want to just fit into your life, I want to build a life; our life together."

Her throat tightened, but she smiled into him.

He kissed her hair, slow and sure. "Let's make this ours. For good."

Outside, the lamppost flickered once and steadied. Maplewick, listening as always, approved.

Chapter Twenty-Three

Some mornings asked you to rise quietly; others insisted you join the chorus. The morning after the festival was the latter. The square was already alive with sweeping brooms, clattering ladders, and the faint smell of cider reheating for breakfast. Mavis walked with Julian at her side toward The Knittery, where her family had made it tradition that post-festival mornings were for yarn, pastries, and a collective exhale in the form of a family gathering.

Julian carried a paper bag of Susan's scones like he was bringing tribute to a monarch. "Is it always this organized after chaos?" he asked.

"Organized?" Mavis laughed. "This is us pretending we're organized. Really, it's gossip and knitting with snacks."

Inside, The Knittery smelled like wool, spiced with clove from the pot of cider Lydia had left steaming on the counter. The long table was already spread with skeins in autumn colors—russet, gold, pumpkin, moss—and half-finished scarves trailed like banners.

Agnes looked up from her corner chair, needles clicking. "You're late," she said cheerfully, though the clock had only just reached nine.

"Brought reinforcements," Julian said, holding out the bag.

That earned him an approving sniff from Irene, who was unwrapping her own project, a knitted garland of tiny acorns. "Smart man. Knows the currency."

Ruth breezed in from the kitchenette door, carrying two extra mugs. "And I've got cinnamon tea. Bribery all around."

Julian pulled out a chair beside Mavis, trying not to look like a man still slightly dazed from the fact that he'd woken up in her bed only hours ago, hurrying back to the inn to change and not be seen by Max. They had agreed on that.

He leaned into the rhythm of it instead; the low hum of conversation, the snick of needles, the occasional burst of laughter when someone dropped a stitch and blamed the cider.

Across the table, Lydia was helping Sophie and Lillian how to cast on stitches, patient as a schoolteacher. Benji and Max sat on the rug with scraps of yarn, attempting to "weave" something that looked more like a fishing net for dolls. Jonah, lanky and amused, supervised with the air of a boy who had outgrown yarn crafts but not his cousins.

The room was full, alive. The kind of full Julian had been chasing without knowing it.

"Now," Agnes said, peering over her spectacles, "let's talk about this historian we've all acquired."

Mavis groaned. "Do we have to?"

"Yes," Irene said briskly. "It's tradition. Knit, sip, interrogate."

From the sofa, Owen raised his hand like a man on trial. "For the record, my interrogation lasted three hours and included a written portion."

Peter, leaning against the doorframe with a mug, nodded gravely. "Mine had diagrams. And a bonus round called 'How good are you with shelf brackets.' Failed the bracket question. Still married Lydia, but I'm on probation."

The room dissolved into laughter.

"Don't scare him," Nell said, though she was smiling.

Julian lifted his hands in mock surrender. "Interrogate away. I've survived worse than knitters."

"Unlikely," Ruth muttered, pouring cider.

The questions came in cheerful succession—Where are you from? (Boston, by way of everywhere.) Do you cook? (Only things that can be eaten with a spoon.) Do you intend to keep distracting Mavis when she's meant to be shelving inventory? (Guilty, unrepentant.)

The room laughed again. Even Max, who piped up: "What's your favorite candy? (Candy Corn, delivered with a wink at Max.)

"Well done," Agnes said, handing him a deep brown, soft wool hat. "You'll need this soon — I noticed you don't have one."

"Mavis reached for another skein just as the air shifted— cooler, like someone had opened a window. A hush pressed in, not unfriendly, just familiar. The cousins barely blinked. The aunts paused, needles poised mid-air. Julian frowned, adjusting his collar. "Draft?"

"Not exactly," Mavis said softly, glancing toward the far corner.

And then they appeared—two shapes, faint at first, like the shimmer on hot pavement, then clearer. June and Beatrix, their sweaters and amused eyes as vivid as if they'd just walked in from the square.

Julian froze. His rational brain staged a small protest, but his eyes didn't move away. He saw them. Really saw them.

Beatrix folded her arms. "Well, it's about time."

June smiled at Mavis. "Told you he'd be one of us eventually."

The knitting needles kept clicking, as if the living and the not-so-living alike had agreed this wasn't worth dropping a stitch over. Agnes gave the tiniest nod of approval. Irene winked.

Julian opened his mouth, closed it again, then whispered, "You're—"

"Ghosts," Beatrix supplied, brisk. "Family. You'll get used to it."

Mavis's hand brushed his under the table. Her eyes were warm, steady. "Welcome to Maplewick," she said softly.

The circle carried on, warm as lamplight, proving that in Maplewick even an interrogation could feel like a celebration. As needles clicked and ghosts whispered their approval, Mavis caught Julian's glance and knew he'd already been knitted in.

Epilogue

By early October, Julian Everett had a house key in his pocket. A real one. Not a guest key from a hotel, not a temporary inn room tag—an iron key on a brass ring, weighty enough to feel permanent. He had bought the pale-green house at the bend of Willow Street, the one with the apple tree leaning over the fence. The porch slanted, the roof needed love, but when he unlocked it for the first time, the windows sighed like they'd been waiting.

He still traveled—notes to collect, archives to haunt—but now his compass was set. Every train ticket had a return date stamped with Maplewick.

In the bookshop, the back office had rearranged itself the way old buildings sometimes did, as if conceding: fine, you can have a desk here too. By winter, Julian's maps lay rolled in the corner, his typewriter perched companionably beside Mavis's ledgers. Max took this as natural law, the same way he took for granted that Julian would test candy jars, fix squeaky hinges, and read drafts of essays about the Revolutionary War with unfeigned interest.

And one evening, when Julian came out of that back office, stretching his shoulders, he greeted Hattie without thinking. "Evening," he said casually, passing her as she worked on shelving a pile of books.

Mavis froze. Then smiled, she was still getting used to him being a true Maplewickian.

჻ ჻ ჻

As October got underway, Maplewick had traded its festival clothes for Halloween finery. The square bore no trace of September's bunting or cider cups—every last scrap swept away weeks ago. In their place, the shops had donned witches' hats and grinning jack-o'-lanterns. Hearth & Bloom had a black-cat display that looked suspiciously like Nibs had posed for it. A scarecrow lounged rakishly against the post office rail, the inn's windowsill pumpkins each wore a different expression, from benevolent grin to outright mischief, and decorative bats fluttered in the shop windows.

The last crumbs of the Autumn Festival had been swept away, replaced with skeletons standing guard in front of businesses, their elaborate scenes waiting to be judged in the Halloween contest. Each business had staged its own elaborate scene for the annual Skeleton Contest—set to be judged on Halloween night. One skeleton in front of the General Store leaned on a broom as if sweeping leaves with grave determination. Another sat at the diner counter, fork in bony hand, eternally deciding between pie and pancakes. The bookshop's skeleton, courtesy of Max's creativity, wore oversized glasses and a scarf, bent over a dictionary as though it had just discovered Latin roots. Voting ballots were stacked at every storefront, and the whole town buzzed with good-natured whispered predictions.

In the back of her mind Mavis knew there were lists waiting—retreat menus, guest bundles, timetables scribbled in Ruth's neat hand. Maplewick didn't stop at one celebration; it kept weaving the next, like a quilt never quite finished.

Julian asked Mavis to walk with him at dusk, when the lamplight pooled warm against the cobblestones. The air smelled of woodsmoke and sugared almonds thanks to Ruth's new recipe. Max skipped ahead, crunching leaves under his sneakers with the focus of a ten-year-old on a mission.

Julian laced his fingers with Mavis's as they crossed the square. "You know," he said, tilting his head toward the hair salon's skeleton band on the corner, "I'm starting to think this town doesn't believe in off-seasons."

"That's Maplewick," Mavis said, fondly. "One long holiday."

At the bend of Willow Street, they stopped before the pale-green house with the crooked porch rail and the apple tree leaning protectively over its fence. Julian rested his hand on the gate, looking at the house like a man already imagining holidays and mornings inside it. He stood for a moment looking at the wide porch and enough rooms for books and for Max's Lego cities. He took a breath, then turned toward her, eyes serious but full. "Move in with me? You and Max. I want this to be home. Our home."

Her heart leapt and she stood for a minute—she hadn't been expecting this.

Julian pulled a solid, brass key from his pocket and held it out to her. "Just so you know," he said softly. "I don't just want you in my life," he said, his voice certain now. "I want you with me. Always. You and Max are my home."

Max whipped around from his leaf pile, eyes huge, grin wider than any pumpkin in the square. "Say yes, Mom!" he burst out, bouncing on the porch step like he might launch into orbit.

Mavis laughed, startled and teary at once, undone by how right it felt. For all the magic she'd grown up knowing, she had never expected this particular miracle: someone asking not just for her, but for both of them. She looked from Julian's open, unguarded face to Max's shining one, and knew.

"Yes," she whispered, the word steady and sure. "Yes." Tears blurred her eyes as she nodded, and when he placed the key in her palm, the town itself seemed to hold its breath, then sigh in approval.

Max whooped from the porch.

Julian kissed her there on the crooked porch, under the apple tree and the glow of lamplight. Maplewick leaned closer, listening.

And then, because this town could never resist, the bookshop lanterns across the square flickered brighter—Hattie's delighted hand at work. In the stillness just after, a familiar brisk voice carried faint on the breeze: "About time," Aunt Bea muttered, tart with satisfaction.

Julian kissed Mavis again, grinning into it, and when they broke apart he said, low and certain, "Guess that means everyone knows."

"Good," Mavis whispered back and laughed, cheeks warm, her heart brighter than the lanterns. And from the square, making their way toward the house, came her whole family.

Lydia and Peter walked arm in arm, Lydia carrying a jar of clove and orange that would simmer on the stove and make the whole place smell like welcome, while Peter balanced a basket of kindling under the other.

Agnes and Irene followed, knitting bags swinging at their elbows, and between them they carried a length of autumn-colored bunting, ready to drape across the porch so the house would look as loved on the outside as it felt within.

Ruth and Susan brought up the middle, Susan steady with a tray of steaming teapots while Ruth carried a basket of warm rolls and cinnamon twists that left a fragrant trail behind them. Ivy skipped between them, proudly clutching a packet of extra sugar cubes, while Benji tried to sneak another roll with frosting still on his cheek.

Bringing up the rear were Nell and Owen, their three children orbiting them like small moons—Jonah with his dependable flashlight, Sophie with a notebook already scribbled full, and little Lillian carrying a sprig of marigolds plucked from the garden. Owen held the family clipboard while Nell kept a pen poised, full of ideas about paint swatches, curtains, and what furniture would best invite people to stay a while.

It was the Maplewick way: home wasn't left to chance, it was made—stitched, brewed, baked, and written into being.

Mavis stood at the gate with Julian beside her, his hand finding hers as if it belonged there, and she felt it down to her bones: this wasn't just her town, her story anymore. It was theirs. A family weaving itself closer, lantern light catching in every smile.

Julian leaned a little closer, his voice low, meant only for her. "I've been a lot of places," he said, his thumb brushing across her knuckles. "But this feels like the first time I've come home."

Mavis's heart lifted, warmer than the lamplight spilling across the square. She squeezed his hand, letting the truth of it settle between them.

Inside, the talk soon turned to plans as it often did with this family. Agnes unrolled an heirloom quilted runner across the kitchen table while Ruth put the kettle on, and Lydia produced a candle that somehow smelled just like the bakery. Nell had already taken herself for a tour of the house to take inventory. And though the Autumn Festival had only just passed, the cousins were making lists of blankets and quilts needed, books to bring over from the shop, tea blends to stock the kitchen with, and creating a menu for a housewarming dinner with the same energy and joy they'd just brought to lantern walks and cider booths.

As the night wound down and coats were fetched from hooks, Ruth snapped her clipboard shut with theatrical flair. "Don't get too cozy—we've got caramel apple

s to test and pumpkins to wrangle tomorrow. Halloween waits for no one."

The kitchen erupted in laughter, but outside the lamplight winked and stretched across the square like it knew a secret.

Maplewick's oldest mischief was waking from a century's nap—and Ruth was about to learn how to play its game.

Acknowledgments

Thank you to my Baba, who taught me the heart of coziness, the gift of comfort, and the beauty of real faith. To Nannie and Bapa thank you for instilling in us the importance of family and the strength of sticking together.

To my brother, Luka—for being the encourager of creativity in our family, and the person I've always known I could count on.

To my Aunt Sarah and Aunt Linda—for being the loudest cheerleaders and biggest support team anyone could hope for. Your unwavering belief in me means more than words can hold. To my Uncle Don—for all the walks to the bookstore and the conversations about what we're reading, those moments are stitched into my heart forever. And to my Uncle Brian—for being so proud and protective of both me and Smith.

To my mom, who gave me my love of reading and never once said no to a new book. And to my dad, who left us too early—I hope the ghostly threads of this story reflect what I've learned: that people stay with us, whether or not we can see them. Our relationships don't end, they simply change shape. I miss you both very much.

To my friends—for the portion of you who are happiest under blankets with tea and books right beside me, and for the portion who still love me even when I choose cocoa over cocktails. You love me for who I am, and I adore you for it.

And to my longtime readers from my blogging and Book Riot days—thank you for reminding me that stories matter, and always being up for discussing them.

And of course, to Smith—you're the best chapter in my story. I love you on repeat forever.

Also by Wallace Yovetich

Coming October 2025: Maplewick Book 2
Coming December 2025: Maplewick Book 3
Coming February 2026: Maplewick Book 4

Want more cozy magic and updates about upcoming books?
Join my newsletter for updates and bonus content:
subscribepage.io/R29jEJ

About the Author

Wallace Yovetich has been a teacher for the better part of twenty years, a book blogger, and a contributing editor at Book Riot. A lifelong reader, she now writes cozy, heartwarming small-town romances with a touch of magic. When she isn't writing, she can be found curled up with a novel and a cup of tea. She lives in Southern California with her family, and more books than she has shelves for.

Visit her at www.wallaceyovetich.com, or on Instagram @wallaceyovetichwrites

www.ingramcontent.com/pod-product-compliance
Lightning Source LLC
Chambersburg PA
CBHW020325200626
46814CB00006BB/2415